Aurore of the Yukon

Aurore of the Yukon

A Girl's Adventure in the Klondike Gold Rush

MacBride Museum Yukon Kids Series

Keith Halliday

Illustrations by Aline Halliday and Kieran Halliday

iUniverse, Inc.

New York Lincoln Shanghai

Aurore of the Yukon
A Girl's Adventure in the Klondike Gold Rush

iUniverse books may be ordered through booksellers or by contacting:

iUniverse
2021 Pine Lake Road, Suite 100
Lincoln, NE 68512
www.iuniverse.com
1-800-Authors (1-800-288-4677)

ISBN-13: 978-0-595-39546-0 (pbk)
ISBN-13: 978-0-595-83943-8 (ebk)
ISBN-10: 0-595-39546-5 (pbk)
ISBN-10: 0-595-83943-6 (ebk)

Printed in the United States of America

To my two Alines

Contents

Foreword

This is the story of a nine year old girl from Montreal named Aurore Cossinet and her adventure to the Yukon at the height of the Klondike Gold Rush in 1898. Amazingly, the story is based on her own diary and is written in her own words.

Aurore's story was recently discovered by her great-granddaughter, Aline. The papers were in a trunk at the old family cabin at Army Beach, tucked in a beautifully preserved copy of the 1899 Girl's Own Annual. There was also a remarkable letter of commendation from Superintendent Sam Steele, the famous Gold Rush era policeman.

Aurore wrote the story for the 1899 Whitehorse School essay contest, and the Annual was her prize. She appears to have kept it for her entire life.

When you read her story, you will see why. It is an amazing tale of adventure, hardship, tragedy and the joy at beginning a new life in the Yukon.

Aurore went on to be a much-loved figure in Whitehorse until her death at the age of 96 in 1986, but the details of her remarkable journey to the Yukon during the Klondike Gold Rush were unknown until now. In particular, Jack London readers will be fascinated to learn that Aurore gave him the idea for *Call of the Wild*, and that the dog "Buck" was based on Aurore's dog. Also, Aurore's first hand account of Soapy Smith and his gang is amazing, not to mention her role in the famous Broadway gunfight in Skagway in which Soapy Smith died.

We have done a minimum of editing to Aurore's story. We have corrected some spelling errors and have updated the place names: Whitehorse instead of White Horse, for example. We have also included the corrections of Mr. Galpin, Aurore's 3rd Grade teacher, as well as a few historical notes of our own. They appear as footnotes in the version you are about to read. We also included some drawings from Aurore's 1899 scrapbook, such as a scene of her hiding from Soapy Smith before the shootout.

Finally, we have added notes and photos in each chapter from Aline's modern-day scrapbook. After Aline discovered the story, she and her family retraced Great-grandmother Aurore's adventure more than 100 years later. Aline's experiences today along the Chilkoot Trail and Yukon River underline the extraordinary hardship and adventure of Aurore's trip to the Yukon.

We hope you will enjoy the tale, and see why Mr. Galpin gave First Prize to Aurore at Whitehorse School back in June 1899.

Professor H.I. Story
Whitehorse, Yukon Territory
2006

Chapter 1

We leave Montreal and home forever

"Why do we have to move to the Yukon? I don't even know where it is!"

—My diary, Montreal, Quebec. April 18, 1898

The first time I saw the word "Yukon" was on a letter that came the morning Papa died. And the first time I heard anyone say "Yukon" was that night, when Maman told us we were moving there.

"Fantastique! Nous allons au Yukon!" exclaimed Yves, my very silly six year old brother. He ran off to get his most prized possessions, his Three Musketeers hat and sword, as if we were leaving in five minutes. I don't think he'd ever heard of the Yukon in his life.

Maman must have noticed the look on my face. "Mais Yves est d'accord, ma chouette," she said.

"Of course Yves thinks it's a good idea, Maman!" I shouted. "He'd be even more excited if you told him we were moving to France to join the King's Musketeers."

Then I ran to my bed. "Mais, ma chouette!" I heard her call behind me. She always calls me "ma chouette" when she's trying to soften me up. Even today. She has never quite been able to learn English. In French, a chouette is a cute kind of owl. That probably sounds funny to you, but it is quite sweet in French.

Anyway, it's not easy to sulk in a small house in the East End of Montreal. I ran to my bed, but I couldn't stay there very long since I shared a room with Yves and my stupid cousin from Trois Rivières. I was soon back downstairs where I found out that we really were moving to the Yukon.

I should have been more thoughtful about Maman's feelings. After all, Papa had just died. He had been sick ever since Christmas. And Maman had been through a lot. I didn't realize how much until that night when I snuck downstairs after bedtime and listened to the adults.

The door to the sitting room was closed, since it was chilly and we only had a fireplace in that room. I lay down on the floor and pressed my ear to the door. It was just Maman and Tante Josephine, Maman's sister. Tante Josephine was much older than Maman. Yves and I were terribly scared of her. She was so strict.

I could only overhear bits of the conversation. They talked a lot about "The Depression,"[1] which is when it is really hard for people to get jobs. I knew this because everyone in Montreal had been talking like that since I was little.

Tante Josephine talked about money a lot. Maman didn't say much. I think Papa took care of the money. Before he died, that is.

I guess Papa had a good job at the Railway and got paid well every week. But now that would stop. Papa didn't have any life insurance, which is where the insurance company gives money to your family if you die all of a sudden. Even worse, I found out that we were in debt. We didn't even own our house. The Bank did!

I must have gasped, since they stopped talking for a moment. I lay totally still, and eventually they started talking again.

---

1.   Good point, Aurore. The depression that started in 1893 was the worst in 30 years. One reason so many people went to the Klondike looking for gold was because they couldn't find jobs at home.—Mr. Galpin

Tante Josephine said we had a big mortgage on the house, which means that we borrowed money from the Bank to buy the house. If we didn't pay it back, they could take the house away.

Has anyone ever talked about taking your house away? It's scary, let me tell you.

Maman and Tante Josephine couldn't figure out where we could get enough money from. Any job Maman could get wouldn't pay much and, anyway, who would take care of Yves and me?

As for our family, Papa didn't get along with his two sisters in Gaspé. They wouldn't be much help. He didn't have any brothers. Maman had seven older brothers, but one had just been injured at the mill and two others could barely support their families. Another one we weren't even supposed to talk about, since he drank too much and was always in trouble. I wasn't even supposed to know about him. My favorite, Uncle Armand, had just gone to sea to go whaling and no one knew when he would come back. Number six worked in the mines in Ontario but had just lost his job in the Depression.

That's when Maman showed Tante Josephine the letter from brother number seven in the Yukon.

I'll never forget what Tante Josephine said. She sort of gasped: "Thibault!" Then she said, "A ranch!" and after that she said a bunch of words that the nuns at convent school don't even say if they burn themselves on the woodstove.

I burst into the room. "It's not fair. Why did <u>my</u> Papa have to die? Why do we have to move to the Yukon? I don't even know where it is!"

Maman and Tante Josephine just stared at me and didn't say anything. They were too surprised to scold me.

I pointed my finger right at Tante Josephine.

"And why do we have to have so many relatives if they can't help us. All they do is bug us at church, pinching my cheeks and complaining when Yves is naughty. Why can't just one of you be rich?!"

Maman jumped up and grabbed me. I tried to run back to my room, but she held onto me and hugged me tight. I could see Tante Josephine sitting in the rocking chair, totally still and looking at us. I think she was crying too.

Aline's Diary #1. Whitehorse. May 1st, 2006

Well, after I found my great-grandmother Aurore's story in that trunk, everyone has been telling me I should start my own diary. This is it. It's just that I can't quite think what to write.

I was over at my grandmother's today. I love her, but sometimes it gets pretty boring listening to all those old stories. Again and again. She's got boxes and boxes of photos upstairs. Plus, she always thinks I can't wait to eat canned peaches with canned milk. I guess it was a real treat in the old days, but looks pretty disgusting now. I'd rather eat a Kiwi fruit or something.

Map of the Yukon Territory. Arctic Ocean. Alaska (U.S.A.). The Yukon. North West Territories. Yukon River. Dawson City. Kirkman Creek. Chilkoot Trail. Pacific Ocean. White Horse. Bennett, Skagway and Dyea.

Aurore's route on the Chilkoot Trail and Yukon River from Skagway to Dawson City.

- Aurore Cossinet
Mr. Galpern's class

Ever since I found Aurore's story, she's had a new burst of energy. Today she came up with the idea that we should retrace Aurore's footsteps to learn about the family history. My Dad heard the idea, and now he's all enthusiastic, too.

I was supposed to go to a sleep over at Kayley's. Now he's dragging me to Skagway, Alaska instead.

He's given me a map that Aurore drew when she was 9. It shows her route from Skagway to Dawson City and back to Whitehorse.

I've been to those places lots of times. The thing I just realized about the map, though, is that it doesn't have any roads on it. My Dad says Aurore had to walk or ride a canoe ... "without a DVD player" he said when I asked where my favorite disk was.
– Aline

Chapter 2

Ho for the Klondike!

"They've painted 'Ho for the Klondike' all over the ship. I guess the Klondike is the part of the Yukon where the gold is. Everyone thinks they'll be rich soon, even the boy who washes the ship's dishes. It's like a big party for everyone except me."

—My diary, on board SS Alpha on the Pacific Ocean.
June 11, 1898

We almost missed our train leaving Montreal. It was because of Yves.

Our train was supposed to be very early in the morning. Tante Josephine and our cousins came to see us off at the station. It was odd to be up so early. The city looks different and everything feels a bit strange.

We had been to the station a hundred times before to see Papa. We knew lots of the men that worked there. They were always friendly.

But this time was different. Everyone acted strangely as they loaded our trunks onto the train. It was like we were going to Africa and they never expected to see us again.

Maman kept talking about Uncle Thibault. And the Klondike. About the big ranch he talked about in his letter. About the "lodge" and the "guest house" and the gold in the creek behind the ranch. About how he said anyone in the family was welcome.

Suddenly, Maman noticed that Yves was gone. "His sword and hat are gone too," I said.

The usual adult panic started. We all ran around looking frantically for him. Tante Josephine was saying something about kidnappers, but no one was listening to her. The conductor was shouting "All Aboard!" just like in stories.

Then I realized where he would be. I ran to the place behind a big pillar where Papa used to take us when he wanted to smoke a cigarette. Yves was there, with his sword and his big floppy Musketeer hat pulled down over his eyes.

"Je ne veux pas y aller!" he sobbed.

"I don't want to go either," I told him. But there was no time for me to cry too. Eventually, I got him to come back to Maman by promising to read him his favorite part of the Three Musketeers. It's the part where D'Artagnan first meets the Musketeers and they become friends after a fight with the Cardinal's Guards. I've practically got it memorized, I've read it to him so many times. I also told him I'd take him to see the conductor.

You've got to do these kinds of things when you have to take care of a six year old brother.

Everyone made a big fuss when we got back, especially the conductor. He said the train was leaving any minute, so we hugged everyone and Maman shooed us onto our train car.

Fortunately, Yves quickly forgot to be sad. We had been to the station before, but we had never been on a train. Pretty soon, Yves was running around exploring closets and poking his nose in other people's cabins. He got so excited that he started waving his sword at the conductor and shouting "En garde" until Maman took it away.

I was expecting a very fancy train, since I had just seen pictures in one of Maman's magazines about Princess Louise's visit to Scotland.

She was with her father the Prince of Wales and all kinds of important Dukes and Duchesses. Princess Louise had a big dress with a hat covered in feathers, and she was sitting in a train car that looked like it was a room in a castle.

But Maman said that we were in Second Class.

Second class is O.K. Our train car was nice, with soft seats, lots of nice wood panelling and big windows. But it was crowded. Yves and I snuck up to see First Class, which looked just like in the photo of Princess Louise. There was even a fancy restaurant car which reminded me of the restaurant beside the train station, with big tables, tablecloths and waiters in white coats.

We didn't go to Third Class, since Maman said it wasn't proper.

Back in our car, the women's and kids' bathroom was at one end, and the men's was at the other. The men were supposed to do their smoking at that end, too.

We had a little compartment with four neat little beds that folded down. On our side, the bottom bed was for Maman and the top one was for Yves and me. I was supposed to sleep on the outside so Yves wouldn't fall off.

The other two beds belonged to a couple of English women. They didn't speak French, but they were very nice. One gave us little Scottish shortbread cookies from a little tin she had in her bag.

I knew quite a few English words which Papa had taught me when I visited him at the railway station, so I said "Thank you." Yves just tried to grab a second cookie. Maman slapped his wrist.

"Si tu n'es pas sage, le conducteur va te mettre sur le toit," said Maman. When she said it, she put a big smile on her face so the English ladies wouldn't know that she was scolding Yves. It's not polite to threaten to put your children on the train roof in public.

Yves didn't really believe that the conductor would make him ride on the roof if he wasn't good, but he wasn't sure. He was pretty good with the English ladies after that.

It took us almost a week to get to Vancouver. Canada is very big. The English ladies showed us where we were on their map as we went along. They ran out of shortbread in Northern Ontario, but the train stopped in Winnipeg and they got some more.

To pass the time, they started to teach English words to us, and would give Yves more shortbread if he learned a really hard word. Yves and I learned lots of English, but Maman had trouble. She couldn't say the English sound "th" at all. Yves used to make fun of her by putting his fingers in his ears and sticking his tongue out while he said "th, th, th, th." She was also always getting things confused, like how she said "Good night" to the conductor every morning when we woke up.

There was also a lot of confusion with the ticket collectors. They came twice a day and Maman always seemed to be showing them the wrong ticket. The English ladies would try to help, but they didn't speak French. Maman would never listen to me, since she thinks that children shouldn't interfere in important things like train tickets. It was very annoying seeing the adults mess it all up again and again.

Every day, Yves and I were amazed by something new. First, by how big Ontario was. It went on for days. And then there were the prairies. How flat they were! After that, wow, the Rocky Mountains going straight up into the clouds.

As we got close to Vancouver, Maman and the conductor had another confusing conversation about how we could get from the train to our ship, the SS Alpha.

While Maman and the conductor were talking in the corridor, one of the English ladies put her hand on my arm. Actually, I had learned their names by then. It was Mrs. Macgregor.

"Are you going all the way to the Yukon Territory? With no one to meet you in Vancouver?" she asked. I could tell she was worried that Maman didn't speak English.

"Yes, madame," I said in English. "My Uncle Thibault says many French Canadians in the Yukon Territory."

She smiled, a bit uncertainly I thought. "That's a very good sentence, my dear. You could hardly speak at all when we started in Montreal." She looked up and checked if my mother was watching. Then she reached into her purse and put something cold and hard into my hand. "I think a girl in the Yukon can always use one of these."

It was a lady's pocket knife, with a Scottish bird and the words "Famous Grouse" printed on the handle.

In Vancouver, Maman was able to explain to a carriage driver where we needed to go. Well, I think it was mostly the note that Mrs. Macgregor gave her that did it. Anyway, we were soon standing on the dock beside the SS Alpha.

Have you ever been on an ocean liner? With the tall smokestacks, the handsome captain and the giant ballroom? Well, those are the ocean liners that go from Montreal to England. The ones that go to Alaska are different.

The SS Alpha was built even before Maman was born. It had three tall masts, with a black hull and white on top. The captain's wheelhouse and the cabins on the deck looked nice…from far away. The ship probably looked lovely when it was first launched in the old days. But now the paint was peeling and it was covered with rust.[1]

The mood on the dock was excited. Everyone was shouting and running back and forth. On the side of the ship, someone had painted the words "Ho for the Klondike," which means "Hurray! Let's go," or something like that. The passengers were carrying all kinds of boxes and bags of supplies. Yves almost got knocked over by a porter with a huge pile of boxes marked "Ammunition." There were about 20 cows on deck, covering the whole back part of the deck

---

1. You are very lucky Aurore! Just after your trip, some of the crew deserted because of safety problems. The ship sank with her captain and eight others off Vancouver Island!—Mr. Galpin

where the passengers were usually supposed to play shuffleboard and other ship games. One part of the upper deck was even reserved for dogs. There must have been 50 of them and they howled the whole time we were in Vancouver.

We had a small cabin again, not much bigger than on the train. It was on the main deck, and we could see outside through a tiny porthole. At first, it looked like we might have all four beds to ourselves. But at the last minute, two women came in. They were joking loudly and I couldn't really understand their English. Their clothes smelled like cigarette smoke and their breath had a strange smell. I don't know what it was, but I saw Maman frown when she smelled it.

"Gosh, you're a brown-eyed little cutie! Gonna be a lady-killer when you grow up, I reckon," one of them exclaimed to Yves. He has a twinkle in his eye that everyone loves. Plus Maman never let anyone cut his hair, so he looked like the Little Prince in that painting. The lady pinched his cheek. "Gosh, and French too," she said, winking at me.

They were a few years younger than Maman and were dressed in very fancy clothes. Not like Princess Louise and her friends in my picture, but like the ladies in the posters outside the music hall in Montreal. I think they were dancers.

The Chilkoot Trail
33 miles
by Aurore C.

Lake Bennett

The End
Bennett
mile 33

Lake Lindeman

Lindeman City
Mile 26

Long Lake

The Border →

Canada Gate

United States

Happy Camp
Mile 21

Snow

Summit with Mounted Police
Tent. Mile 17

The Golden Stairs (steep)

Sheep Camp
Mile 12

Mud and Floods →

The Start.
Dyea - Mile O

Skagway

Pacific Ocean

Aline's Diary.#2. Whitehorse. May 9th, 2006

Our first trip to Skagway ended up being pretty interesting, although I missed the sleep over *and* a trip to the movies.

We drove to Dyea, where the Chilkoot Trail starts. Aurore hiked it with her mother and brother, so next month we're going to retrace her steps and hike the Chilkoot Trail too. I was worried my Dad was going to make me wear an old fashioned dress like Aurore did, but he says I can wear my shorts.

Here's a map of the trail that Aurore drew. It's 33 miles long, or 53 kilometres. The mountains are huge... just look at the photo below! Don't get the idea that there are lots of towns along the way. Guess how many people live in Dyea, Lindeman City and Bennett? Zero. They're ghost towns today.

– Aline

I got this picture at the MacBride Museum. It's Skagway after the Gold Rush.

Photo courtesy of the MacBride Museum (1985-39-183)

The tall one was beautiful and her eyes and smile seemed to be like a magnet. You couldn't forget them.

"And what about you, Missie?" she said to me as she unpacked. "My name's Kitty Rockwell, from Junction City, Kansas.[2,3] Pleased to meet you, miss!" She kept unpacking, turning to smile at me from time to time. "Now don't you have a pretty little dress and beautiful long brown hair and big blue eyes?" She gave me a long purple ribbon and said it was for my hair. "That black hair thing you got ain't pretty at all, sweetie."

"Qu'est-ce qu'elle dit?" demanded Maman suspiciously. She couldn't understand what we were saying but wanted to know. Then Maman shooed us into bed and got out her book, a sure sign she wanted to ignore our new cabin-mates. Eventually, they went out. We could hear them laughing with the other passengers in the hallway.

I don't think Maman enjoyed the trip from Vancouver to Skagway. She wouldn't let us wander around like she had on the train. Not that we could go anywhere, what with the dog pen and all the cows on the deck. The people on the ship were much louder. Long after we went to bed, we could still hear shouting and laughing from the restaurant beside us.

We went to the restaurant in the morning. Sometimes there were even men sleeping outside the door when we got there. Our eggs and toast always took a long time, usually because our waiter was so busy cleaning up beer bottles from the night before.

As we sailed North, it seemed like the mountains kept getting bigger.[4] The days kept getting longer. In the North in the summertime, the sun stays up almost all night long. They call it the "midnight sun." One night, we got to stay up to 10p.m. Maman didn't realize how late it was until a man stumbled out of the restaurant and fell down

---

2.   Editor's Note: Remarkably, it appears Aurore met Kitty Rockwell before people started to call her "Klondike Kate." There were at least several other "Klondike Kates" in the Yukon but Kitty Rockwell was the most famous as a popular Dawson City dancer and singer. Her meeting with Aurore seems to be a year earlier than historians had previously thought she got to the North.

3.   Editor's Note: Using modern scanning technology, a blacked-out comment by Mr. Galpin can been read here on the original paper: "I know what you mean about magnetic eyes..." Historians are unable to confirm exactly what he meant by this.

4.   They were, Aurore. We covered this in geography. Seven of ten of Canada's biggest mountains are in the Yukon.—Mr. Galpin

in front of us. Then Maman hurried us back to our cabin. She didn't even punish Yves for shouting "Take that!" and poking the man with his wooden sword as he lay on the floor.

We didn't see much of Kitty and her friend. They would stay out late, even after midnight, and then come back and make a lot of noise going to bed. They would usually sleep late the next day, so that Yves and I would have to be quiet until lunchtime. One morning, Kitty's friend was even seasick in our cabin even though it wasn't stormy at all outside.

Maman didn't think our cabin-mates were proper. Or the other passengers. Or the crew. Or even the Captain, whose crumpled uniform didn't look half as important as the conductor on the train. She must have said, "Ce n'est pas correct" a hundred times during our voyage.

Of course, Yves and I thought it was all kind of fun.

Chapter 3

Maman, is this really Skagway, Alaska?

"I didn't know you could call a place a town if all the buildings are really just tents."

—My diary, Skagway, Alaska. June 17, 1898

We woke up to find the SS Alpha anchored off Skagway, Alaska. I don't know if you've heard of Skagway. I think the whole world has heard of it by now, thanks to the story of Skagway, Dyea and the Chilkoot Trail.

The best way to get to the Klondike gold fields in the Yukon is by either the Chilkoot Pass or the White Pass. The Chilkoot Pass starts at Dyea and the White Pass at Skagway. Two years ago, the only people living there were Captain Moore and his family. They had a little house near the beach at Skagway.

Then they found gold in the Yukon creeks and the Gold Rush started. Thousands of people sold everything and went to the Yukon hoping to get rich. The poor Moore family had thousands of people camping on their farm![1] That was the year before we got there.

---

1.   Be precise, Aurore. It was 10,000 people through Skagway in 1897 and the same at Dyea. Even more came in 1898, the year you were there.—Mr. Galpin

Over the winter, thousands of people had been packing their supplies up the trails into the Yukon. The Chilkoot is the steepest but the shortest. The problem was that the North-West Mounted Police were scared that there wouldn't be enough food in the Yukon, so they said you couldn't cross into Canada unless you had a year's worth of supplies. That's nearly 2000 pounds! That means 40 trips back and forth if you could carry 50 pounds a time!

So that's why Skagway and Dyea are now the biggest towns in that part of Alaska. When we arrived, there were still thousands of people going back and forth over the passes with their stuff. Plus, there were new people like us arriving every day.

Maman's plan was to get the train from Skagway to the Yukon.

"Why is everyone else hiking the Chilkoot if there's a train?" I asked. But Maman told me to shush. Our first problem was getting off the boat. The dock in Skagway was so busy that there was no space for our ship to tie up. Instead of making us wait with the cows, the Captain was nice enough to lower the ship's boat. We and the other passengers took turns as the boat took us and our things to shore.

The little boat finally got us and our trunks to the dock. It was like the dock in Vancouver, but even worse. There were people running all over the place. There were dogs everywhere. There were healthy looking dogs just off the boat. There were more dogs tied up in teams, howling and barking. And there were dogs just running loose in every direction. The noise and bustle were amazing. Maman tried to ask for help. "Excusez-moi! Pardon!" she said, in French of course. People either ignored us or just looked at us funny.

I guess we did look pretty funny. A nice lady in a proper dress, with an eight year old girl and a small boy with a wooden sword dressed in a French sailor outfit. Maman loved to make Yves wear that sailor outfit. Anyway, we also had three big trunks that none of us could lift. All around us were husky dogs, regular dogs, boxes, bags of flour and a lot of busy men.

"Où sont les carrosses?" asked Maman.

"I don't think there are any carriages," I said. "And where would one take us? I don't see any buildings!"

There actually were buildings, but mostly it was just tents. Even stranger, some of the buildings were just tents with walls built around them.

Suddenly, Maman reached out and tapped a man on the shoulder as he was walking by. She pointed at the pin on his suit. I recognized it right away. It was the same pin that Papa's best English friend at the train station in Montreal always wore. The pin had three circles linked together. They were white, red and blue. The club was called "Oddfellows."

He smiled at us. I liked him right away. He was a tall man with a gray[2] beard and little round glasses. He had a big belly, but not too big, that stuck out of his suit. He was dressed more nicely than the other men, who mostly wore working clothes.

He reminded me of Father Christmas at Mr. Eaton's store in Montreal at Christmastime.

"Clancy Cicero at your service, ma'am," he said with a little bow.

Maman pointed at his pin again. Papa had always said that it was a good club. English, but still pretty good. They used to raise money for the hospital and help each other if anyone got into trouble.

Too bad Papa wasn't a member.

Mr. Cicero even spoke a little bit of French. He was very helpful. He whistled and, before we could say a thing, two other men had appeared and were loading our trunks onto a cart. Then we walked up Broadway street to a hotel where they said there was room for us. The railway tracks went right up the middle of Broadway, but I didn't see any trains.

---

2.   GREY, not GRAY. No American spelling, Aurore. We spell the proper British way at Whitehorse School.—Mr. Galpin.

The hotel was called the Royal Palace Hotel. This sounds pretty fancy, but it was really just five tents with boards laid in the mud in between so you didn't get too dirty going from the front tent to your own in the yard behind. The St. James Hotel was just down the street. It was actually made of wood.

Three of the Royal Palace's tents were for people to stay in. One was the office. And the fifth was the restaurant. That's what Maman called it, but I heard Mr. Cicero call it the "bar."

The man who checked us into the hotel was very nice. "More Friends of the Eagles?" he asked Mr. Cicero.

Mr. Cicero coughed. "No Jim. I'm an Oddfellow! You know that!"

The man seemed embarrassed and didn't say anything more.

We were feeling much better now that we had a place to stay, even if it was just a tent. Maman tried to ask Mr. Cicero some questions. His French wasn't very good, so she got me to help too. First Maman explained our plan to get to the Yukon.

"By train!" exclaimed Mr. Cicero. "Why, the track is only finished two miles out of town. It won't be done until next year![3] If you want to get to the Yukon, you'll have to walk over the Chilkoot Pass, take a boat from Bennett to Whitehorse, cross the rapids, and then take another boat from there to Dawson City. It's almost 500 miles!"

When I translated this to Maman, she made me ask him again and translate the answer another time.

We wouldn't have been more surprised if Mr. Cicero had told us we had to sprout wings and fly over the Chilkoot Pass.

"Don't worry, ma'am," said Mr. Cicero. "I'll come back in a few hours. I'll take you to the telegraph office so you can send a message back home saying you and the kids are safe."

Maman was so shocked she didn't even say no when I asked to take Yves back to the dock to throw rocks in the water.

---

3.   Done in a year! It didn't even get to Carcross in a year...and that's
      only halfway!—Mr. Galpin

Yves and I were throwing rocks and watching all the people come and go when Yves saw a man beside a boat talking to a dog. There were three men in the boat watching as the man squatted and rubbed the dog's head. Rope and a club lay at his feet. The man seemed strange. Sad. Serious. Nervous.

You could tell the dog was a special kind of dog. He wasn't a little house dog like Tante Josephine had. He looked like he was half St. Bernard and half shepherd. He was big. Bigger than me. He was majestic. And there was something in his face that told you he was smart. I think he knew, just like Yves and I knew right away, that the man was about to do something bad.

I picked up a stick and said "en garde" to Yves. Yves caught on right away. He drew his sword and play-fought with me to push me back, closer to the man. Suddenly, we could hear the words.

"Look fella," the man said. "I can't take you back. I've only got enough money left for myself." The dog looked at him, then glanced at me and Yves. "In fact, I really need money bad." Suddenly, the man flipped the rope over the dog's neck. The dog jumped back, but it was too late. The rope was tight around his neck, but gosh how the dog struggled. He was so big, the man could barely control him. The dog was like a wild animal, a huge wolf like its ancestors.

The man hit the dog three times with the club, hard. I had never seen anyone hit a dog so hard before. The dog yelped and I gasped, since I was afraid the dog would be killed.

But the dog still barked, and tried to bite the man and get away.

"Quick," shouted one of the men in the boat. "Go sell him to Quinlan before he gets away! The ship's leavin' in 5 minutes."

The man raised the club to strike again. I bit my lip and looked away.

I was waiting for the blow to fall, when suddenly Yves jumped past me. His wooden sword swished through the air and came down right on the man's knuckles. The man yelped and dropped the rope. It was just for a second, but the dog was gone.

The man cursed and swung his club at Yves. I gasped as Yves ducked and the club swished by his head. It was so close it knocked off his hat.

Yves and the dog ran straight past me. The man chased after, shouting, "You rascal! I'll have your hide for that!"

Even one of the Three Musketeers needs help sometimes, so as the man passed I hiked up my skirt and stuck out my leg. The man tripped all over the sand. Before he could get up, I ran off as fast as I could. Something landed near me. A bottle, I think. Probably thrown by the men in the boat. But when I looked back they weren't chasing us.

"Get back in the boat, you loser!" laughed one of the men. "The ship's leaving this hell-hole in 5 minutes!"

"Yeah! It's not like you lost money on him. You stole him from Judge Miller in the first place!" shouted another. The man with the club threw it in our direction. We watched as they rowed the boat out to a ship. Finally, they went up the ship's ladder and just kicked the boat away. I guess they really were leaving Alaska.[4]

Anyway, Yves and the dog came out from behind some willows as soon as it was safe. The dog licked my hand and rubbed his head on my leg. Yves rubbed his neck.

"What should we call him?" I asked Yves.

"D'Artagnan, after my favourite musketeer," was the immediate reply.

---

4.   Thousands of men turned back before they went over the passes. In many cases, they were the most fortunate.—Mr. Galpin

Photo courtesy of the MacBride Museum. (#3944 29)

Aline's Diary #3. Whitehorse. May 18th, 2006

I visited my grandmother today. She asked about all these places in Skagway, but I don't think they exist any more. She gave me this photo of Skagway in the old days. Look at the mud in the streets!

Things are a lot different today. Except for our hotel. There wasn't a bathtub in our room. I think maybe the sheets and blankets were from the Gold Rush too.

My Dad took me to the beach in Skagway. We watched the seals play in the sun and threw rocks into the ocean.

He showed me this picture that Yves drew of the very same spot. It was where they saved their dog D'Artagnan from those mean men.

It was kind of strange to think that I was playing in the same spot that my great-grandmother played on.

– Aline

On the Beach in Skagway (by Yves writing by Aline)
with D'Artagnan

Chapter 4

A telegram from Soapy Smith

"Big fire at the house. Please send money for doctor as soon as you can."

—Telegram from my Aunt Josephine. Received in Skagway, Alaska. June 29, 1898

Yves and I took D'Artagnan back to our hotel. Well, back to our tent. Maman was waiting for us. At first she wanted us to give D'Artagnan to someone else, but Yves and I begged to keep him. Finally, she agreed to let us keep him, but just for one week.

We saw Kitty and her friend trudge by carrying backpacks. They waved and said they were headed for the Chilkoot. Yves and I went outside to play with D'Artagnan in the alley beside the tent.

I'll never forget that moment. The sun was bright and warm and there were no clouds in the Alaskan sky. It was perfectly blue. The air was so clear you could see the snowy mountains around Skagway like through a telescope. All around us Alaska was growing as fast as it could, around the clock in the midnight sun. The grass was long and the rhubarb was taller than me!

I even remember the smells. One minute, the rich hot air was full of the smell of Alaskan trees. The next minute, a puff of cooler air from the mountains that smelled as clean as a glacier.

There was a young man sitting in front of the tent beside ours. He was leaning back in the sun with his boots in the air. He was about 20 years old and was slim and handsome, with a big bit of uncombed hair that just fell across his forehead. He had bush clothes on, which means the kind of clothes you would wear carrying your gear over the Chilkoot.

When he saw me looking at him, he smiled. "That's a great dog you've got there. He'll make a great sled dog. Can I throw a stick for him?"

He said his name was Jack London.[1] When you looked closer at him, you could see he didn't look as healthy as a young man should. He was even missing a few teeth. But he was in good spirits and threw the stick for the dog.

---

1.   Editor's Note: Aurore's story adds a whole new dimension to Jack London's story in the Yukon. Historian Dick North has traced him to Skagway in August 1897, then over the Chilkoot and to Dawson City by October. He was actually 21 at the time, not 20 as Aurore guessed.

Until Aurore's story came to light, it had been believed that the dog "Buck" from Jack London's Call of the Wild was based on a dog in Dawson City. This dog was named "Jack" and belonged to Marshall Bond, whose cabin was near the spot where Jack London pitched his tent. Interestingly, London also borrows Aurore's story about the dog having been stolen from "Judge Miller" in California (see Chapter 3).

London later staked a claim on the Left Fork of Henderson Creek. Aurore's story is the first report that he came back to Skagway in 1898. Previously, it was believed that he had floated down the Yukon River to its mouth on the Bering Strait on his way back to California. His first winter on Henderson Creek had been very tough, with London contracting scurvy and losing several teeth from lack of vitamin C.

Jack London didn't get rich in the Yukon. According to some documents, when he cashed in his gold back in San Francisco it was only worth $4. As he floated down to the Bering Straight, however, they say that he spent all his spare time scribbling stories in his notebook. These stories would make him the wealthiest author in the world within ten years.

D'Artagnan loved to fetch sticks. Mr. London could throw far. Every time, D'Artagnan would get the stick. "C'mon! Bring it to Jack!" he would shout. But D'Artagnan would always bring it back to Yves or me.

"I was gonna offer to buy him from you, but it looks like he likes you guys too much!" said Jack with a laugh. I was already getting to know the different English accents. Jack sounded American, like Kitty. Not at all like Mrs Macgregor.

Yves and I told Jack the story of the man with the club.

"Is that right?" He seemed very interested, especially in the part about D'Artagnan being stolen from a judge's house in California and becoming so wild as he fought with the man. "I think you're right, Miss. Think of a dog leaving the big city and coming to Alaska. A dog would change right away. Why, it's the law of club and fang up here. The very heart of the primordial." I had to write that word down in my diary and look it up later. It means something that has been around since the start of the world. Alaska feels like that, as if it is the place where things are still wild, like they were everywhere before people came. Jack was quiet for a moment, like he was thinking.

"Sometimes he just stands and stares into the mountains," I said as we looked at D'Artagnan. "It's like he can hear the wild calling him."

"That's exactly it, Miss. The call of the wild. What a story that dog could tell!" he said finally.

Jack started telling us stories. He was the best story teller I had ever heard! There was one about a woman named Mercedes and her friends. They left Skagway with an overloaded sled and not enough dogs and didn't know what they were doing. They weren't careful and went right through the ice of the Yukon River. They were never seen again!

Jack called them "Cheechakos," which means newcomers to the North country. Oldtimers are called Sourdoughs.

Yves and I were so caught up in the story, we didn't even hear another man walk up beside us. "Are you Jack London?"

"You bet," smiled Jack.

"I'm Frank Reid, the town surveyor." He looked grim, like a school teacher dealing with a bad kid. "They told me you were at my office. What's this I hear about you wanting the deeds to One-Eye McCallion's land on the other end of Broadway?"

"Oh, no, sir! I don't want the deeds. One-Eye's brother is coming up on the boat from Seattle next week. The land is for him. One-Eye thinks he should stay in Skagway and start a store instead of risking his skin in the Klondike."

"Well, where's One-Eye?"

"Stuck down in Dawson City after a nasty wrestle with a bear! But that's another story. I promised him I'd come up to Skagway and bring the paperwork."

Are you wondering why he said "down in Dawson" and "up to Skagway" when if you look at a map, Dawson is at the top and Skagway is at the bottom? It's because you travel by river in the Yukon, and Dawson is downstream. Everyone would know you were a Cheeckako if you said you were going "up" to Dawson.

Anyway, Jack reached into his tent and grabbed a big envelope. "I've got a whole bundle of legal papers from a fancy lawyer in Dawson City for you. They should back up the story. I just brought them here as a favour for One-Eye. I reckon he saved my life on Henderson Creek last winter."

This seemed to make Mr. Reid feel better. "I heard there was a fellow on Henderson Creek who kept the miners entertained all winter with stories about all manner of things." He smiled at Yves and waved his cane at him like a sword as he talked to us. "Well, it's a pleasure to meet you, Mr. London. I was just afraid you were one of these con men. The town's full of them."

I forgot to ask Maman that night what a "con man" was. I don't think she would have known. Anyway, we found out ourselves soon enough.

~   ~   ~

Just after Mr. Reid left, Mr. Cicero showed up. It was almost like he'd been waiting for Mr. Reid to go.

"Well, my friends, it's time I lived up to my promise to take you to the Telegraph Office. Your family must be worried sick about whether you made it safely to Alaska."

We walked down Broadway. Just as we were passing a building marked "Jeff Smith's Parlor," a man in a big hat stepped out. He had a black beard and a big round hat. He had a nice vest and a suit. But it was his eyes that I remember. They were small and seemed to look at you hard for a minute, then jump away to someone else.

"Hello Soapy!" said Mr. Cicero.

"Headed for the Telegraph Office, I hope," said Soapy, almost with a snarl.

"You bet! Nice day for it!" said Mr. Cicero quickly.

Soapy looked at us. He put on a fake smile and said, "Hello children," in a fairy tale sort of voice. I could tell he was the kind of man who thinks kids are stupid.

"Good afternoon Mr. Soapy," said Yves.

"Let's go kids," said Mr. Cicero.

We of course asked Mr. Cicero who Soapy was. His real name was Jeff Smith[2]. Soapy was just a nickname.

---

2.   Editor's Note: Jefferson Randall "Soapy" Smith. His nickname came from a scheme to avoid a law against lotteries in Colorado. He put a $100 bill inside one package of soap in a basket. People could pay to "buy" a bar of soap in the hope of finding the $100. The Colorado policeman who arrested him forgot his first name and entered "Soapy Smith" in the police log.

"How did he know we were going to the Telegraph Office?" I asked.

Mr. Cicero stuttered for a moment, which was unusual. "Well, err, he's a businessman and, umm, businessmen need to know everything that's going on."

"And why do they call him Soapy?" asked Yves.

"Err, you'll have to ask him that yourself."

The Dominion Telegraph Office looked like the most permanent building in Skagway. Even the bank seemed like just a tent with wood stuck on the outside, in comparison. There was a great big pole right in front, with wires that snaked behind Broadway towards the water.

"Mr. Cicero," I asked. "Did they really put wires under the ocean all the way to Vancouver so we can send telegrams?"

"You bet, sweetie," he said. "They've got one between New York and London under a whole ocean, so I guess Skagway to Vancouver isn't too far. Sure is handy though."

In the office, they were very nice. It was expensive. They charge you for each word so you have to write short messages. Ours was just eight words. In English, it translated to just seven: "We safe Skagway. Leave for Yukon soon." The clerk was a boy a few years older than me. They called him Jimmy "Blackball" Houlihan.

I don't know why everyone in Alaska has to have a nickname, but they do.

Blackball asked us lots of questions to make sure he had the address right and the names of the people we were sending it to. Then he even let us watch as he sent it to Vancouver. He tapped it out on a machine in what they call Morse Code. Each letter has a combination of dots and dashes. An "e" is one dot. An "a" is dot-dash. A "k" is dash-dot-dash. So our message sounded like just a lot of clicks.

"The telegraph office in Vancouver can understand it too," said Blackball. "They write it down and then sent it to the next city, and so on, until it gets to your Aunt Josephine in Montreal."

As we left, Mr. Cicero smiled at Blackball. "Good job, boy," he said.

~   ~   ~

We waited in Skagway for awhile as Maman tried to figure out how we were going to get to Uncle Thibault's if there wasn't a train.

Sometimes Maman would send me to the Telegraph Office to see if our family in Montreal had written us back. Finally, one day, there was a message. Blackball gave me a fancy Dominion Telegraph envelope made of nice paper. I ran back to our tent and gave the envelope to Maman.

She opened the envelope, then shrieked and dropped it to the ground. Yves grabbed it, but he couldn't read, so I snatched it from him. "Grand feu maison. Envoyez monnaie vite pour hopital."

In English, this would read something like, "Big fire house. Send money fast for hospital." It was signed by Tante Josephine.

The telegram put all of us in a tizzy. "Which house? Who got hurt? Why do they need money?" I asked. But Maman didn't know of course. The telegram was all we had and Montreal was 5000 miles away.

Maman rushed down to the Telegraph Office and sent home most of our money. She also sent a long and expensive message with our questions and sending our prayers.

The first telegram had only taken 2 days to get to Montreal and come back. But we waited for days and days this time and didn't hear anything. "I hope they are OK," I would say at night to Yves. Sometimes, when Maman was asleep, I would read the telegram again. There was something strange about it. Tante Josephine was very proper, but the French in the telegram was very bad.

Maybe she was trying to use fewer words, I wondered. But on the other hand, some of the words just seemed wrong. For example, "monnaie" in French doesn't mean "money" in English. "Monnaie" means "coins." And you wouldn't really say "feu" for a house fire. A proper person would say "incendie."

I told this to Yves, but he just said that Tante Josephine must have been even more upset than the time he broke her special plate with a picture of Queen Victoria on it. Even though Tante Josephine was French-Canadian, she loved Queen Victoria.

~   ~   ~

We were still waiting when the 4th of July came. This is Independence Day in America and they have big parades everywhere, even places like Skagway.

Yves and I ran down to Broadway to get a good spot. We stood right in front of the Red Onion Saloon, which is the best place to be if you ever go to the 4th of July Parade in Skagway. It's the best spot because there is a good bench and you are close enough to the beginning of the parade that everyone in it still has candy to throw to kids.

The person leading the parade turned out to be Soapy Smith, Mr. Cicero's friend. He gave us another fake smile and threw some candy. He was wearing a big sash that said "Grand Marshall of Skagway."[3]

Behind him was a banner for the Skagway Benevolent Fund, which Soapy had set up to help widows and orphans of men killed on the Chilkoot.

---

3.   Editor's Note: Aurore doesn't mention it, but Soapy had formed his own "Committee for Permanent Law and Order" to head off Frank Reid. Soapy paid or threatened 300 people into joining and making him "Grand Marshall." He also paid for a brass band to follow him down the street during the parade.

"Grand Marshall of Skagway!" exclaimed a deep voice right beside us. It was Frank Reid. He spit into the road. "The ice will freeze in H-" Suddenly he noticed us and stopped. He smiled like a guilty man. "Err, umm, Hawaii. The ice'll freeze in Hawaii before Soapy Smith is fit to be any town's Grand Marshall!"

"But he's Mr. Cicero's friend!" said Yves.

"Yes," I said. "We met him on our way to the Telegraph Office with Mr. Cicero."

"Cicero and Soapy Smith! Those two are in cahoots!" That's an Alaskan word that means people who do bad things together.[4] He suddenly froze. "Did you say you went to the Telegraph Office?"

I quickly told him about the fire and how Maman sent our money back to Montreal.

"That's the last straw! Widows and children! He's got it backwards with his Benevolent Fund. You're supposed to give your money to the widows, not the other way around," he exclaimed. I don't think I've ever seen anyone so angry before. Not stamping his feet and shouting at you. Just quiet and determined. Fiercely angry. "I've got to talk to your Mama, kids. The wire coming out of that Telegraph Office doesn't go to Seattle or Vancouver, it's just tied to a stump down by the water."

Without saying another word, he stomped across Broadway. He went straight through the parade without looking left or right, almost knocking over the fellow carrying the "Liarsville Friends of the Eagles Lodge" sign. I watched as he spoke to two other men, then all three of them walked quickly away.

---

4.   Actually, "cahoots" is American slang and was first used in 1829. It appears that no widows or orphans ever got any money from Soapy Smith's Widows and Orphans Fund—Mr. Galpin.

Aline's Diary #4. Whitehorse. May 24th, 2006

My class went to the MacBride Museum today. Our teacher gave me this photo of Soapy Smith. He did such terrible things, but everyone talks about him like he was a hero. I guess bad guys are more interesting ... as long as you're reading about them and not getting robbed by them.

This shows the inside of his saloon and some of his gang members. Too bad Blackball isn't in the photo, but I wonder if that's Windy Bill in the background. And I think I can see the door at the back where Aurore hides ... whoops, that's the next chapter!

－ Aline

Photo courtesy of the MacBride Museum (1989-1-119)

Chapter 5

Gunfight on Broadway

"She's just a girl."
—Soapy Smith describing me. My diary, Skagway Alaska.
July 8, 1898

So much happened in the days after the July 4th Parade. Frank Reid told Maman that the Dominion Telegraph Office was a fake and that all our money had been stolen by Soapy Smith and Mr. Cicero.

Actually, he had to tell me, and I had to tell Maman. It was quite a scene. Maman cried all night long. When Yves and I tried to comfort her, it just made her even sadder. I think she thought she was a bad mother for getting us kids mixed up in everything. Mothers are like that sometimes, I think, even though they try their best and really do such a good job of taking care of you.

Mr. Reid also talked to the other people in Skagway who weren't in Soapy Smith's gang. They formed a group called the Committee of 101 to "clean up" Skagway and get rid of Soapy and his "lambs." That's what Soapy called his gang members. Soapy also had his own committee, called the Committee of Permanent Law and Order. Soapy wasn't really interested in law and order, of course. It was just one of his many tricks. Most of the people on it had either been paid money or threatened into joining, I think.

I guess Soapy had been tricking Cheechakos for a long time. Besides the Telegraph Office, he also had Jeff Smith's Parlor. It wasn't very big, but it had a bar and a casino, which means that people could gamble and play games for money. Soapy's lambs would give Cheechakos free drinks. The men would get drunk and then Soapy would either cheat them at gambling or steal their money. Soapy also had a freight service, where they would charge you money to send your boxes to Seattle. Then they would just steal what was inside or dump your boxes in the ocean.

Soapy was a rough man. Sometimes, if you didn't fall for any of his tricks, he would tell his men to "take you out to see the eagles." That meant they'd take you to the edge of town and beat you up and steal your money.

Mr. Cicero was also a famous con man[1]. His specialty was exactly how he tricked us with his Oddfellows pin. He would wait on the Skagway dock looking for men with club pins, like the Oddfellows. I guess he had 50 different pins in the cigarette case he kept in his jacket pocket, from the Mason's Club[2], Friends of the Eagles, Order of Foresters and so on. He knew each club's secret handshake too. When he spotted a man wearing a club pin, he would put on the same one and pretend to bump into him. Then he would make friends and take the fellow to the Telegraph Office or another Soapy Smith trick.

I didn't like Soapy Smith from the second I met him. But Mr. Cicero had been really nice. He completely fooled us.

Mr. Reid's friends were really nice to us once they found out what had happened. They moved us out of our tent right away. I guess Soapy owned the Royal Palace Hotel and had been over-charging

---

1. Editor's Note: There are no known historical references to Mr. Cicero, although several of Soapy's accomplices were known to use the tricks Mr. Cicero used. Others pretended to be doctors or reporters in order to meet Cheechakos on the Skagway docks.
2. Aurore, it is the Masonic Lodge, not Mason's Club. And it is not a club, but a serious fraternal order with high ideals.—Mr. Galpin.

us. We moved into another tent behind Mr. Reid's house. Everyone was always bringing us Sourdough pancakes, bacon, Alaska blueberry pie and all kinds of things. Mr. Reid said Yves looked like a baby grizzly bear with its face covered in blueberry stains all day long.

All this time, Soapy Smith pretended that nothing had happened. He walked up and down the middle of Broadway just like he did before. But not quite so many people said hello as before, and some even crossed the street to avoid him.

July 8th was a bad day. That was the day we found out that Soapy Smith told Mr. Reid that he wouldn't give our money back. He said we were making it up, even though Maman had a little receipt from the Telegraph Office. Maman wanted to call the police.

"We don't have the Mounted Police here like they do in Canada," said Mr. Reid. "The nearest police are one hundred miles away in Juneau."

"We have to fix this ourselves," said one of Mr. Reid's friends. "Soapy just stole $2600 from a miner yesterday. We've got to fix that too." Then they went off to another one of their Committee of 101 meetings.

"What do they do at their meetings?" asked Yves.

"Not much, it looks like," I replied.

~　　　~　　　~

That afternoon, I decided to get our money back myself. Maman and Mr. Reid hadn't got it back, and I knew exactly where Soapy's headquarters was.

Yves and I had played Three Musketeers all over Skagway. We knew the town as well as anybody.

I explained the plan carefully to Yves. He would hide in the giant Alaska rhubarb behind Jeff Smith's Parlor, which was Soapy's headquarters. I would bring a bench and climb in through the tiny window on the back wall. It was too small for an adult to get through and they left it open most of the time. We had looked in the front window lots of times. I knew the window either went into Soapy's office or a storage room. Then I would get back as much of our money as I could and climb back out.

If I got caught, Yves was supposed to go get Mr. Reid. I also made a backup plan for what I would do if I got caught. If I had a chance to get to the front door, I would try to run. If I didn't, I would say I was just trying to steal more candy. I had one piece left from the parade and I put it in my pocket.

It's always a good idea to have backup plans. I learned that from reading the Three Musketeers to Yves about 300 times.

I was scared—really scared—as I climbed up to the window. There was a piece of string stopping it from opening all the way, so I pulled out Mrs. Macgregor's knife and carefully cut through it. Then I opened the window all the way. I could see inside the storeroom. I checked that no one was in it and then climbed through the window. I got a nasty scrape on my leg and landed with a thump.

It sounded so loud that my first thought was to jump back out the window again. But no one seemed to have heard me or to care. There are a lot of things in Alaska that go "thump."

I looked through the key hole into the Parlor. There were a few men sitting at the bar drinking beer. I crouched down so no one could see me and slowly pushed the door open. I waited for someone to say something like "Hey! Who left that door open?"

When no one said anything, I quickly crawled into Soapy's office.

His office had two comfortable chairs and a desk. It was filled with all kinds of junk. "Most of it's probably stolen," I whispered to myself. On his desk was a gun and a set of gold scales. There was so much gold from the Klondike around, that lots of people paid for things with little bags of gold instead of money. That meant you had to weigh it.

I pulled open Soapy's drawer. There were two sets of weights for the scale there. They looked the same, but one set had little holes drilled in the bottom of each weight.[3]

But no matter where I looked, there was no money or gold. It must have all been in the safe under the desk. I looked around for a combination written on a piece of paper but couldn't find one. And even if I had, I thought, I don't know how to open a safe!

Suddenly, the front door of the Parlor banged. "Soapy! I thought you were at Clancy's Bar!" said the bartender.

"Give me a beer," snarled Soapy in return. Then he started looking for his gang. "Where's Cicero? Where's Windy Bill[4] and the rest of my lambs?"

"Should be here any minute."

"OK. The rest of you, clear out!" There was a scraping noise as the other customers left the Parlor. Soon, they were replaced by Mr. Cicero, Blackball and the rest of Soapy's gang.

I was in a total panic. There was no window in Soapy's office, and no way I could get back to the storeroom without getting spotted. Rather than do something foolish, I decided to hide. I crawled down under Soapy's desk and pulled in the chair to hide my legs.

Have you ever had to hide? Not just from your brother, but from really bad people? It's horrible. For a minute, I started to cry. But I had to stop. I would get caught for sure!

From under Soapy's desk, I discovered that I could see through a crack into the main room of the Parlor. Skagway buildings are so badly built that their walls are always crooked and cracked. I could see Soapy, Mr. Cicero, Blackball as well as fellows like Windy Bill and the rest of Soapy's gang. Windy Bill seemed to be looking right at

3. Editor's Note: Soapy was playing an old trick. By drilling holes in the weights he made them a bit lighter. That way, people would think Soapy was giving them an ounce of gold but they would really get less.
4. Editor's Note: Robert Service mentions Windy Bill as one of Soapy's gang in his poem "Montreal Maree."

me through the crack. My heart started to go even faster. He was one of Soapy's meanest friends. He never smiled and always acted tough, even tougher than the rest of the lambs. Fortunately, I realized he couldn't possibly see me through the crack. He must have been looking at something on the wall. I calmed down a bit, but not too much. I was still trapped in Soapy's office with no escape, after all!

Soapy was talking. "Frank Reid is ruining this town," he said. The others nodded. It looked like they always agreed with whatever Soapy said. "All these do-gooders. Whiners! Who cares if a few Cheechakos get fleeced? Don't they know what we've done for Skagway."

"Put it on the map," said Mr. Cicero.

"Yeah!" said Blackball. "The Juneau newspaper says Skagway is the most lawless town in Alaska!"

This made Soapy mad. "Shut up, Blackball. That's not what I meant. We've got the Committee of Permanent Law and Order. That's 300 people on our side. Who does Frank Reid think he is anyway?" said Soapy.

"What are you going to do, Soapy? Frank Reid has called a meeting on the docks."

"What? That dirty dog. Always interfering in other people's business." I heard the sound of Soapy smashing his glass on the floor. "Tell the lambs to get over here. And bring their guns. We'll shoot Frank Reid and break up his precious Committee of 101."

Mr. Cicero spoke up. "Blackball, here's your math lesson for the day. Which is bigger? 300 or 101?"

Everyone laughed and started talking loudly as Mr. Cicero left to get the rest of the lambs. Suddenly, through the crack, I saw Soapy get up and head for the office.

He's going to catch me for sure, I thought. I froze and tried to shrink into the shadows.

But all he did was take a bottle of whisky off the desk and go back into the Parlor. I waited a few more minutes. What should I do? I could wait until they all left, but by then Frank Reid might be dead.

I waited another five minutes to get my courage up, then crawled out from under the desk.

I crept towards the door to see if the storeroom was clear. Suddenly, I found myself staring straight at Blackball's shoes!

I jumped up and tried to run past him, but he tackled me. "Soapy! Look who was in your office!" I begged him to let me go, but Blackball just laughed and pinched my arm in a really mean way. "You're in big trouble now, missy," he hissed, sort of laughing at the same time.

Soapy Smith and the others stared at me. "It's the French girl!" said the bartender. "She must have heard everything."

"Nah. She's just a girl!" exclaimed Windy Bill, banging his beer mug down on the counter. A million thoughts went through my head. I'll never get Maman's money back, I thought. How will I escape?

"Well, she outsmarted you!" replied Soapy with a snarl. "I thought you were supposed to make sure no one could sneak into this place!" He looked at me for a minute. His eyes were hard. I've never seen so much meanness in a person's eyes. My knees started to feel wobbly. I thought I was going to fall down and beg for forgiveness.

But I didn't.

"Yeah, I guess she is just a girl," said Soapy. He didn't sound sure. "I was just in my office a minute ago and she wasn't there. She must have just come in." He turned to me. "How did you get in here?" I pointed at the storeroom window. "When?"

I had no idea what to say, when suddenly I remembered my back up plan. That's why you have back up plans, so they pop into your head when you are too nervous to think of anything on the spot. "Just now, Mr. Smith." I started to cry. "I just wanted some more candy, like you threw at the Parade. I've got just one piece left." I put my hand in my pocket and showed him the last piece of liquorice I had left from the Parade.

"Liar!" said Blackball, but Soapy ignored him.

"I'm all out of candy, missie," he said with that fake smile he uses on kids. "But here's 25 cents. Go buy some more for you and your brother." He gave me a quarter, then shouted, "Now, get lost!"

I ran out of the Parlor, but just as I went through the door, Blackball pushed me. I flew across the sidewalk and went right under a wagon on the street. I was covered in mud and my knees really hurt.

I looked up, to see Blackball in the doorway smirking proudly. "Don't let me catch you around here again, girly!" he said.

I got Yves from the rhubarb patch and we ran as fast as we could to find Mr. Reid. He was at the corner of Broadway and 2nd Avenue talking to a friend.

Breathlessly, we told him what had just happened. "They want to kill you!" I said.

Mr. Reid didn't say anything for a long time. I couldn't tell if he was worried or just thinking. "Bill, go to the dock and tell everybody you see. I've got to get some reinforcements."

"But, Frank, you don't have your gun! Windy Bill or Soapy will just shoot you!"

"But I don't have time to go home. I've got to get help."

"I'll go get it!" I said.

Mr. Reid looked at me for a second, deciding. "OK, Aurore. I can trust you to do a good job. Go to my house. The back door is open and my gun is under my bed. Bring it to the dock." I started to run, but he put his hand on my shoulder. "I never keep a loaded gun around the house. Too dangerous. The bullets are in my bedside drawer." I ran off with Yves trailing behind me.

I was breathless by the time I got there. I yanked open the back door. The gun was in a box under the bed. It was a pistol. I looked at it for a moment. It was scary. I'd never touched a gun before.

Then I grabbed it and dashed out of the house. I was almost to the corner, when I remembered. The bullets! I ran back and yanked open the drawer. I pulled it so hard it came out and fell on the floor. The bullets scattered everywhere. Even worse, there were three different boxes for different kinds of guns.

Which kind fit the pistol in my hand?

I just grabbed a handful of all three kinds and stuffed them into my dress pockets. Then I ran for the dock with my pockets jangling with bullets like I had a handful of pennies for the spring fair!

I got there just in time. For once in Skagway, there was nobody on Broadway. Even the dogs had disappeared. I could see Soapy and the lambs step out of Jeff Smith's Parlor a few blocks away and start walking towards the dock.

The men on the dock standing with Mr. Reid looked scared and nervous. Even Mr. Reid looked white. He put six bullets into the pistol. "Thanks, Aurore. Now, get lost. I mean it. Go see your mother. There might be shooting. I don't want you or Yves to get hurt."

I knew Maman was in our tent writing letters to Montreal. I was about to run there, when suddenly I noticed Soapy just a block away. I grabbed Yves and we jumped behind a pile of boxes near where the dock joined the land. I made him squirm behind some bags of flour and told him not to move.

Mr. Reid shouted at the Committee of 101 and most of the men went onto the dock to have their meeting. He stayed as a guard with 3 other men at the end.

It was totally quiet as Soapy and the lambs walked towards the dock.

"You're not welcome, Soapy," called Mr. Reid.

"We'll see about that," said Soapy. He was wearing two pistols and had a double-barrelled rifle. The rest of the gang had guns too. For the first time, I saw a smile on Windy Bill's face.

Soapy and the gang kept walking towards the dock. One of the men who was supposed to be helping Mr. Reid dropped to his knees and crawled behind the flour sacks like Yves.

The first two guards told Soapy to stop, but they didn't have any guns and he just told them to shut up. Windy Bill gave one a push and laughed.

Mr. Reid seemed to sort of brace himself and said, "Stop right there." It wasn't too loud, but his voice didn't sound afraid.

Soapy said something to Mr. Reid, then raised his rifle. Not to shoot Mr. Reid, but to hit him with the wooden part.

Everything suddenly seemed to be going in slow motion. Mr. Reid blocked the rifle with his arm and pulled his pistol out of his pocket with the other.

"For God's sake man, don't shoot!" I heard the crack of Mr. Reid's pistol, but Soapy didn't flinch. The shot had missed.

Soapy tried to grab Mr. Reid's gun, while Mr. Reid held onto the end of Soapy's rifle. Suddenly, there were two more shots.

Soapy fell backwards onto the ground with his arms flung out wide. He didn't move again. Mr. Reid fell too, but was moaning and holding his lower stomach.

Soapy's gang turned and ran. Blackball and Windy Bill were the first to go. They didn't even stop to help their friend, Soapy.

Everyone else just stood around. They were too shocked to move. I saw blood pouring onto Mr. Reid's shirt. He really looked like he was in pain. The man hiding with Yves behind the flour sacks stuck up his head, but still no one went to help Mr. Reid.

I ran out from my hiding spot towards Mr. Reid. "Come on!" I shouted. I grabbed one of the men's handkerchiefs and pressed it against where the blood was coming from. "Where's the doctor!"

"Right!" shouted one of Mr. Reid's friends, finally. "Let's get him to the nurse."

I looked up. Standing at the corner of Broadway and 1st Avenue was Maman. She was staring at the ruckus in puzzlement. Her eyes went from Soapy Smith, lying still in the middle of the road, to Mr. Reid. Then finally to me. When she recognized me kneeling in the middle of Broadway beside Soapy Smith and Mr. Reid with my hands covered in blood, she fainted, with all her letters to Montreal scattering onto the boardwalk like confetti.[5]

---

5.   Editor's Note: Aurore's version of the shootout is very similar to other historical accounts, even including Soapy's last words and Frank Reid's first shot missing. Reid lived for 12 days before dying of his wounds. He was buried with honour in Skagway Cemetery with a large monument that reads: "He gave his life for the honour of Skagway." Soapy Smith was killed instantly by a bullet in the heart. He was buried outside the cemetery in unconsecrated land.

Aline's Diary #5. Skagway, Alaska. July 5th, 2006

We drove to Skagway today to start our hike on the Chilkoot Trail. I'm missing horse camp at Fish Lake because of it. The July 4th Parade in Skagway was lots of fun. After, we walked up Broadway — where the shootout was — and visited the cemetery. Just like Aurore's story said, Frank Reid has a hero's grave and Soapy Smith doesn't. Most of the tourists wanted to visit Soapy Smith's grave first, though.

Here is a picture that Aurore drew of sneaking into Soapy Smith's office and hiding under the desk. Pretty scary. You can see a gun, and Soapy just outside!

– Aline

Drawing from Aurore's scrapbook.

Chapter 6

My birthday on the Chilkoot Trail

"The boys on the Chilkoot Trail act pretty tough. But they don't have to hike in a skirt."

—My diary, Sheep Camp on the Chilkoot Trail. July 29, 1898

Boy, did I ever get in trouble when Maman recovered from fainting. "Tu n'es pas 'la heroine' de Skagway! Heroine! Plutôt, une petite fille très méchante!"

Yves immediately translated it for the reporter from the Skagway News. "She's not the 'Heroine of Skagway.' She's a very naughty little girl." The reporter had come to our tent after the gunfight to interview me.

You see, after the gunfight, everyone started calling me a heroine for warning Mr. Reid what Soapy Smith's gang was going to do. I even got Mr. Reid's gun for him.

But Maman just shouted in French at the reporter and the other people until they went away. Then she grounded me. She was so upset that she told me I'd have to stay in our tent for the rest of the Gold Rush.

She was very worried that I might have been hurt, of course. But I was pretty mad at her.

"If you hadn't given all our money to Soapy Smith, I wouldn't have had to steal it back!" That's when she said the Gold Rush was too short, and that I was grounded forever.

Anyway, I spent the next few days in our tent doing grammar exercises and reading. Yves and D'Artagnan played in the field outside, which was very annoying. Some nice people brought some books about the Chilkoot Trail and the Yukon for me.

The books were very interesting. One was called *The Klondike and All About It*. It was from New York. It had a list of "Women's Supplies" at the back.[1] I noticed we didn't have very many of the things on the list, like "3 gingham aprons that reach from neck to knees." One of the things listed was even "a man who takes the necessary camping outfit and food along." We definitely didn't have one of those.

"You don't need a man," said Yves. For once, I agreed with him. "You've got me!" he went on, not quite understanding what I meant.

Maman couldn't read the English words but told me not to worry. I kept worrying anyway and wrote the list into my diary.

The other books were interesting too. The funny thing about the Chilkoot and the Yukon is that very few people had ever been there before the Gold Rush. So when the Gold Rush started, people didn't know what to bring or how to live in the North country.

This doesn't count the Native People of course. They had been in Alaska and the Yukon for thousands of years and knew all about the place, not that very many white people bothered to ask them. The worst story I read was about some miners in the Yukon who ran out of fresh food. All they had to eat was bannock, which is a kind of Yukon pancake you make from flour. Pretty soon, they got scurvy from not having any fresh fruit or vegetables. Scurvy makes your gums bleed and your teeth fall out. It can even kill you.

---

1.   Editors' Note: the page with the list of "Women's Supplies" is reproduced from Aurore's diary in the appendix at the back of this book.

By the end of the winter, they were in rough shape. Some Native People told them to make tea from the spruce tree needles all around their cabin, but the miners didn't listen to them.

When the miners finally went to the hospital in Dawson City, they had hardly any teeth left. They must have felt pretty silly when the doctor told them the same thing the Native People had.

Can you imagine? Losing your teeth to scurvy when you were living in the forest surrounded by millions of trees, but not knowing that the spruce needles could save you?

I learned a lot about the Chilkoot while I was grounded. It starts at Dyea. It goes 33 miles to Lake Bennett in Canada. That doesn't seem very far if you're used to travelling by train. But It's a different story if you are walking. The trail goes up more than 3,500 feet into the mountains from the beach. That's just to the "pass," which is the part you walk through. The mountains on either side are twice as high.

And not only is it long and steep, but the trail is very rough. In fact, there is no trail in some places. At the Golden Stairs, which is the steepest part, you just have to crawl over huge rocks that the ice has broken off the mountains.

The day before we were supposed to leave, one of Mr. Reid's friends came over to help us. Her name was Tina. She had blonde hair and bright blue eyes, but the thing you noticed first was the biggest smile I've ever seen. She was so friendly. Mrs. Macgregor was friendly too, but in a quieter way. I don't know how to describe it, but Tina was "Alaska friendly."

She really knew about Alaska and the Yukon. She even had a necklace that her husband had made for her out of 10,000 year old Mammoth ivory. Do you know what that is? It means it is the tusk of an Alaskan elephant that lived before the big Ice Age over 10,000 years ago! It was carved into a beautiful shape like a whale's tale.[2]

Anyway, Tina helped Maman organize her dad Paul to take us to Dyea in his boat. Dyea is the town beside Skagway where the Chilkoot starts. Tina and Paul also arranged for two packers to meet us on the dock in Dyea. Packers are men who carry the heavy stuff over the Chilkoot. People like Jack London carried all their own things over the Chilkoot, but packers usually helped people who weren't as strong.

But you should have seen Tina's face when she saw what we had packed! "Three trunks!" she exclaimed. "You'll never get those over the Chilkoot!" And then, when she saw what was inside, she was horrified. "Six dresses but no winter boots! Well, Aurore, you just tell your mama that this isn't going to work!"

I showed Tina our book, *Klondike and All About It.* Tina took one look and exclaimed, "3 gingham aprons! New York nonsense!" She tossed our book into the fireplace. "That makes your load one pound lighter already!"

Tina's dad Paul just laughed. "I'll show Yves a few card tricks while you ladies repack the gear!" I think Paul had been stuck in lots of snowstorms in cabins with nothing to do, and playing cards is a good way to pass the time. Maman didn't approve of cards, of course, but she didn't say anything. We had bigger problems at the moment!

While Paul taught Yves a few card tricks, Tina, Maman and I went through our three trunks. Tina said we had to be "ruthless," which means making hard decisions about leaving behind things we liked. Tina didn't speak French, so I had to translate most of the talking.

"The first thing is boots. If you wear those fancy shoes, you won't even make it to Sheep Camp!" Tina told Paul and Yves to put down the cards and see if a friend of hers had better boots for us. Then we went through everything and put it in three piles: definitely needed,

---

2.   Editor's Note: fossil ivory carving is still a favourite of Northern artists. During the ice age, some parts of the North were frozen but didn't get enough snow to be glaciated. This allowed many remarkable examples of prehistoric bones to survive to today in the permanently frozen earth. Gold miners in Dawson City continue to find mammoth bones to this day.

definitely not needed, and "Maybe...if we have enough room left-over at the end."

Pretty soon, the "definitely not needed" pile was very big. Blouses. Nice dresses. Our church hats. Maman at first said she wouldn't give up a couple of her dresses. I hated to see my nice red dress on the "definitely not needed" pile. We kept sneaking things back into the "Definitely needed" pile, but Tina would usually catch us.

"Better to leave it here, than carry it halfway up the Chilkoot and throw it out there," she said.

Tina also said that we needed a fourth pile, which was "stuff you'll freeze to death without but don't have any of." She made a list. It included winter boots, wool hats, mitts and good sleeping bags. That was stuff we would need in the winter. She also made a list of the things we would need on the Chilkoot, like food, a pot to cook it in, and matches to light the campfire.

Paul and Yves came back with boots, as well as backpacks to replace the trunks.

We had two packs for the packers we were going to hire. They both weighed 100 pounds. There was a 25 pound pack for Maman. I don't think she'd ever carried a backpack in her life and it made her sway back and forth like a tree with too much snow on the top. My pack weighed 5 pounds. It just had my jacket, a metal canteen full of water, my favourite little doll, a book and my diary. They tried to take my book and diary away, but I snuck them back in.[3]

Paul even gave us a pack for D'Artagnan. Maman was hoping that D'Artagnan could carry some stuff from the "Maybe" pile, but after we put his food in there was only a little bit of space left. A friend of Paul's named Isaac Taylor[4] came by. He was originally from England, but had come to Alaska from another gold rush in Australia! He had a couple of small bells he wanted to give us to scare the

---

3.   Editor's Note: Fortunately for this book!

bears away. He tied one bell on D'Artagnan's collar, and another on my pack.

Yves didn't have to carry anything except his sword. He was too little. I snuck his Musketeer hat into my pack.

The next day, Tina gave one of Mr. Hershey's Milk Chocolate bars to Yves and me. Then Paul and Isaac took us to Dyea where we met our packers.

Our first packer was named Red McGraw. He was from Arkansas. He looked just like you'd expect a tough man from Alaska to look, although I wondered right away if we could trust him. We worried about that with everyone after Mr. Cicero.[5] The other packer was a fellow from the Tlingit tribe, although you actually say it as if you spelled it "Klingit." I couldn't pronounce his real name, so he just told us to call him "Skookum." This is a Tlingit word that means "very strong[6]."

---

4.   Editor's Note: This is Isaac Taylor, who went on with William Drury to found the famous Yukon general merchant and fur trading company called Taylor & Drury. He was working in Skagway on the White Pass railroad in July, 1898, but left in a stampede with almost 1000 other men on August 7th when word of the Atlin gold find reached Skagway. Most took White Pass's shovels and picks with them!

5.   Editor's Note: another remarkable element of Aurore's story, and more evidence of her perceptiveness. Robert Service mentioned a "Red McGraw" in his poem "The Duel." If Service based the story on the same man Aurore describes, then she has good reason to be worried, since "The Duel" portrays Red McGraw as a dishonest sheriff.

6.   Editor's Note: Aurore is probably incorrect throughout her book when she refers to her friends as speaking Tlingit. Most of the words seem to be Chinook Wawa, or what used to be called Chinook Jargon. The MacBride Museum's historical experts tell us that Chinook Jargon is a trade language that was used on the Pacific Coast in the 19th and early 20th centuries, by both Europeans and First Nations. It has a simple grammar, based on Chinook and Nuuchanuulth words, but including some French, other native languages and English. Some Chinook Jargon words have made their way into modern English, such as "potlatch", "high muckymuck," "skookum" and "cheechako."

Aline's Diary #6. Sheep Camp. Chilkoot Trail. July 6th, 2006

The hike has been tiring, but pretty fun. This is me having lunch on the first day. I don't know how Aurore did it in a dress.

– Aline

Skookum had his niece with him. He was taking her across the pass to her grand-mother some-where in the Yukon. She was about my age. The English name she used was Louise, and she had beau-tiful black hair and dark brown eyes with a twinkle in the corner. We were too shy to talk to each other at first, but I could tell that we would be friends.

Louise was very polite and said "How do you do?" to my mother when we were introduced. She spoke no French, but her English was pretty good. She and Skookum spoke Tlingit.

We started at 10 in the morning. Louise led the way, with Red and Skookum right after. The first stop on the trail was Finnegan's Point. It was about 5 miles. Some people go there directly by boat up the Taiya River. But Maman said something about how expensive it was, so we walked.

~   ~   ~

It seemed like we walked forever. Maman said the trail seemed more like a deer trail than a people trail.

"Maman! We're in Alaska. My book says Alaska has more moose than deer!"

Her mouth opened to tell me to be quiet about my book, but instead her foot disappeared into a huge mud hole and she fell over. The mud was so thick it took Louise and me to get her leg out. The mud made a giant "gloop" sound when her foot finally reappeared...without her boot! It took us five minutes to dig out her boot and wash it.

Maman wasn't very happy. Her boot made a squelching sound with every step and she looked funny with one leg coloured mud brown.

We kept walking on the trail up the Taiya River. Sometimes we would walk in silence, just our boots and the bear bells to listen to. Other times, we would sing songs or just talk. Hiking the Chilkoot seems to make it easy to talk. You have lots of time.

Once after a long silence, Yves suddenly said, "Red, my dad is in heaven." Yves says things like that sometimes. Out of the blue. Maman didn't hear him and no one else said anything for awhile.

Then Red said, "My daddy went out for cigarettes when I was eight and never came back."

"Did he get lost?" asked Yves, very concerned.

"Don't think so."

"Then why didn't he come back?"

"Don't know. Maybe 'cause of me and my sister. Maybe 'cause we were so poor."

"Where is he now?"

"Don't know. But if I find him in the Yukon I'll knock him down."

That kept Yves silent, but just for a minute. "My daddy gave me a hug before he went to heaven." This made me start to cry. I remembered that day. It was the day the letter arrived from Uncle Thibault in the Yukon. Papa was lying in bed with his skin as white as the sheets. But Yves wasn't crying. He was just telling Red what happened back in Montreal.

Red thought about what Yves had said for awhile. "You're a lucky boy, kid," was all he said.

After Finnegan's Point, the river was too fast and rocky for boats. The problem was that the mountains went straight down into the river, so usually there was no "shore" along the river. Just mountains going straight up. So the trail had to climb up over big rocks and giant trees. Other Chilkooters had tried to make steps in some places, but sometimes the trail was so steep that Yves had trouble climbing up.

There were lots of people on the trail. Either they were carrying light packs and headed for Dyea, usually with smiles on their faces. Or they were headed to the Yukon with huge packs. There were also horses, mules and every kind of dog you could imagine. The animals didn't look healthy, like you see in the city. They looked skinny and sort of sad.

It was almost all men we passed. They were usually surprised to see a woman. They would take their hats off or say something like "Good morning, ma'am," to Maman. I think they were much politer on the trail than they would have been if we'd been in Skagway! Maman would always reply very politely in French.

Sometimes, the men would stop and talk to us. They were even more surprised to see kids. They would tell us about the trail ahead and would ask us if the water in the creeks was high. Or they would ask us if Soapy Smith was still robbing everyone in Skagway. One time, we started telling some men about the gunfight. Before we knew it, there were thirty men listening to Red and I tell the story of Soapy Smith and Frank Reid. I didn't tell them about me being called the "Heroine of Skagway" since that seemed like bragging.

Red was different. He wasn't even at the gunfight, but he managed to make everyone think he was one of Frank Reid's best friends.

When we were done our story, one man kept talking to us. His name was Percy Brown and he said he was a Major. Red told me later that he had a fancy English accent like the Prince of Wales.

He wore an expensive coat that had a special leather pad on the shoulder for resting your rifle against when you were shooting. He also had strange short pants with boots and stockings. Best of all was his hat, which was like you see in pictures of the British Army in Africa.

One of Skookum's cousins and six other Tlingit porters were carrying his gear. He had a large number of strangely shaped cartons marked "British Museum," not to mention four different fishing rods.[7]

"Madame," he said to Maman. "I do not believe it is dignified for a woman to travel the Chilkoot Trail unaccompanied, especially with impressionable minors. I insist on escorting you back to the city at once." Percy used so many big words I filled up a whole page in my diary writing them down. "Dignified" means "proper" and "impressionable minors" means kids who might see things they weren't supposed to.

When he found out Maman didn't speak English, he said it again in French. Very proper French, in fact. It is even easier to speak down to someone in French than in English. He sounded like a schoolmaster talking to a poorly behaved student.

Maman was surprised for a moment. Then she got mad. She looked him right in the eye and said in her most proper Montreal French, "Monsieur, this family will be dignified wherever it goes. And that includes building a new life at our lodge in the Yukon!"

---

7.   Editor's Note: This appears to be Major Percy Brown, immortalized as the "Piccadilly dude" in Robert Service's *The Ballad of the Ice-Worm Cocktail*. In it, Brown annoys the patrons of the Malamute Saloon in Dawson City by pretending to be a Sourdough. They retaliate by making him drink an Ice-Worm Cocktail, neglecting to tell him that the "worm" is really just a piece of spaghetti.

I was proud of her.

Percy was so surprised he didn't say anything for a second. And when he tried to, another man interrupted. "Ma'am," he said, "I don't know what you said but it sounded like the right thing to me." He stepped right in front of Percy and held out his hand to help Maman up from the stump she was sitting on. He introduced himself as Joe Boyle[8] and said he was headed back to Skagway to get more supplies for his mine in Dawson. "But I'd be happy to help carry your pack for a few miles towards the summit."

He was a big, handsome and very strong man. He put down his pack by the side of the trail, picked up Maman's, and we started walking. Five minutes later, he had Maman's pack, my pack and Yves on his shoulders too.

We all liked him right away, even Maman. He was one of those people you feel like you've known your whole life.

I told him what Maman had said to Major Brown. "Well, that sounds right to me. It's how you act that makes you dignified, not whether you're in the big city or properly escorted." He said "properly escorted" in the same sort of English accent as Percy Brown. He was really good at English accents and told us all about Dawson City as if he was Percy. Louise and I laughed and laughed.

After about two hours, we got to a good resting spot. "Well, I'd better turn around and go get my pack," he said. "Otherwise, I'll be sleeping outside with the bears tonight!"

We all thanked him.

---

8.   Editor's Note: Joe "King of the Klondike" Boyle was from Woodstock, Ontario. He started out fighting boxing matches for money in Dawson City, but soon made a fortune from mining. He convinced the Prime Minister to let him start using giant gold dredges, then organized the famous 1905 Dawson City Nuggets hockey team to challenge for the Stanley Cup. He left the Yukon in 1914 to fight in World War I, where he ended up as a British spy in Russia and helped Queen Marie of Romania save the Crown Jewels and the lives of dozens of Romanian aristocrats.

"Just one question before we go. Now tell your mother that I don't mean to be like Percy the Piccadilly dude, but could you ask her why she's taking two kids into some of the toughest country there is?" I explained about Uncle Thibault and the lodge. He seemed sceptical. "Never mind your uncle. Ask her what the real reason is."

I translated for Maman. She waited a second and looked at me and then at Joe Boyle. I think sometimes being out in a place like the Chilkoot Trail lets you answer questions you never would at home. "Because being poor and trapped in East End Montreal is no way for these two to grow up," she said.

Joe considered this for a minute. Then he smiled and tipped his hat to Maman. Then he turned to me and told me something I'll never forget. "Remember this, Aurore. In the North country, the only thing that can stop you is you. You don't have to worry about being poor, being dignified, being a girl or being whatever. You'll know what to do."

He turned and walked down the trail. As he turned the corner, he looked back and shouted, "Just don't let being 'Heroine of Skagway' go to your head!"

I've never figured out how he knew about that.

It was a lot less fun walking without Joe Boyle to entertain us. Maman and I were scared of bears the whole time, although Yves said he wanted to see one. Louise told us not to worry. There were so many people on the Chilkoot that all the bears had been scared off. I hoped she was right. I was glad we had D'Artagnan and our bells. We made sure to make lots of noise so we wouldn't surprise any bears busy eating berries.

Sometimes the trail was so steep it went along little cliffs. Maman wouldn't let Yves go by himself. She would hold his hand. Other times the trail would go down through swamps. A couple of times, we had to walk right through creeks. There was no bridge! Or if there had been, the floods when the snow melted had wrecked the bridge.

Red called this "fording." We would stop and take off our boots and socks. Then Maman would put our socks on the top of her pack and we would put our boots back on. This was because you couldn't go barefoot across the creeks. They were too rocky.

When you stepped into the creek, the icy water would fill up your boots like lightning. The water was coming from melting glaciers out of sight at the top of the mountains. It was so cold, it felt like your feet were burning even though it was actually cold! Yves asked me if the water was so cold that it would freeze solid if the creek bottom flattened out and the water didn't move as fast.

You had to be very careful. Even if it didn't seem steep, the water was moving so fast that it would pull at your feet. Maman fell once, and I did two or three times because I was smaller. Plus, twice, my skirt got caught on a stick and tripped me up. Yves held onto Maman's hand and was OK, even the time Maman fell.

Then, on the other side of the creek, you would pour the water out of your boots and put your socks back on. Red told us to be careful not to get sticks or sand inside our socks, because then we would get blisters. Your socks would get wet as soon as you put your wet boots on, but they were still drier than if you wore your socks across the creek.

Once, we walked across a swampy part. It was flat and there was a little sidewalk that someone had made out of boards. This is called a boardwalk. It is to keep your boots from sinking deep into the mud. But the problem was that a beaver had built a dam across the creek. The whole area was flooded. So we walked across the boardwalk, but up to our knees in water for five minutes!

After a few scrambles and falling in a creek for the third time, I decided it was time to change out of my skirt. It was always getting in the way, and Louise and Yves seemed to be having a much easier time in pants. I would just wear my long underwear, I decided. This would be much more sensible.

Louise held up a jacket for privacy and I quickly changed. I put my skirt in my pack, put on my long underwear and then put my boots back on. It felt very comfortable. Louise gave me the "thumbs up" sign.

Of course, when Maman saw me standing there in my long underwear pants and big muddy boots, she nearly fainted again.

She made me put on "proper" clothes again, which meant a skirt. Louise and Skookum talked to each other in Tlingit. I think they thought we were very silly.

It was sunny the whole time, but you could hardly tell. This was because the Alaskan trees are so tall! They branch out over your head and their branches form a "canopy," which is like a roof for the forest. There were only a few holes where you could see sun.

Underneath the canopy, it was very wet. Red and Skookum sweated a lot, but it would never dry. Pretty soon their shirts were completely soaked. Plus, it had rained the night before. Lots of flowers and plants called ferns grew along the trail. Their leaves were very wet and as you walked along they would brush against your clothes. So you would be completely wet as if it was raining![9]

When we rested, Louise would show us different kinds of plants. She knew most of the English names even though Maman and I didn't even know the French ones for them! It was very interesting. There was the Sitka spruce and the Cottonwood tree. Then there were beautiful purple flowers called Monk's Hood or Wolfsbane. This is actually deadly poisonous! Then there were lots of different kinds of berries. Worst of all was Devil's Club, which is a big green plant

---

9.   Nice description, Aurore. The Chilkoot Trail passes through three climate areas: the Alaskan rainforest, the Alpine area above the treeline, and the Yukon interior. Each is very different. There aren't very many places where you get three climate zones in 33 miles! We'll study this next year.—Mr. Galpin.

with leaves sort of like a maple tree. But if you touch it, it gives you a terrible rash.

There were also lots of kinds of strange mushrooms and fungus. Some grew out of trees sideways. I thought they look like fairy balconies. Louise didn't know what a fairy was, so I explained all the different kinds to her. She knew about the saints from the missionaries, but had never heard of leprechauns or elves.[10]

We were exhausted by the time we got to Sheep Camp. We had walked 13 miles in two days. I had blisters on both feet. So did Maman. We were completely soaked and muddy. Yves and I fell asleep as soon as Skookum put the canvas down on the ground for our tent.

Maman woke Yves and me up an hour later. She had cooked some nice little bannock cakes on the fire and Louise and Skookum had gone into the forest to get some blueberries to sprinkle on top.

"Bonne anniversaire, ma chouette," said Maman with a sweet smile. It was July 29th! Things had been so exciting that I had forgotten my birthday was coming up. I was nine years old.

Suddenly, I remembered my birthday the year before. Maman, Papa, Yves and I went to the circus and then for a big dinner. That was when I felt the first raindrop.

All of a sudden, I couldn't do anything except start to cry. I just lay down on our canvas groundsheet, put my hands over my face, and sobbed. Yves tried to give a hug, but not even he could cheer me up.

---

10.   Aurore, I don't think Father Ted at your church would be very happy to have you talking about saints and elves as if they were the same sort of thing.—Mr. Galpin.

Chapter 7

The Golden Stairs to Happy Camp

"Hot beans at the top of the Chilkoot are the best lunch in the world!"

—My diary, Happy Camp on the Chilkoot Trail. July 30, 1898

The clouds were hanging low over Sheep Camp the next morning. Really low. It was like the sky had been lowered.

Sheep Camp was almost like a little town. It had restaurants and hotels and even a tramway that they had built from Sheep Camp right to the top of the Chilkoot Pass. It even had two streets and there were hundreds of people. I even thought I saw Blackball for a minute.

Using the tramway would have been nice, but we had hardly any money left. In fact, the night before while I was asleep Red McGraw had asked Maman for more money to carry our packs. I guess packers did this a lot. They would agree to one price in Dyea. Then, once you were desperate, they would ask for more.

A few weeks in Alaska had made Maman tougher. You could see it when she talked to people like Red McGraw. Even though Maman's English was bad, she was able to explain to Red that we didn't have much more money and that she wouldn't give him any more.

When we woke, we found out that maybe she shouldn't have told him that. Yves was the first to figure it out. When he woke up, he jumped out of bed and ran over to the tree where Red and Skookum were.

"Where's Red?" he asked. Skookum woke up and looked around. His face had a "Oh no, not again," look on it. It turned out that Red had disappeared. When it started to rain and he found out we didn't have any more money, he snuck back to Dyea.

"At least he didn't take the pack," I said.

"No, just the food," replied Skookum.

I think we all wanted to cry at that point, maybe even Skookum. But Maman was very brave. She said we would keep going to Uncle Thibault's no matter what!

Maman grabbed the packs. We had to redo Tina's three piles, since we only had one packer left! Skookum agreed to carry a heavier pack. Louise did too. Louise knew all about dog packs and tied some clever knots so that we could fit a bit more onto D'Artagnan. I agreed to carry some of the food. But still, we had to leave a lot of things behind like spare clothes.

We hiked out of Sheep Camp. We had 5 miles to go to get to the summit of the Chilkoot. After that, it starts going down out of the mountains on the other side. Maman made us sing French Canadian songs to keep us happy. I taught Louise how to sing *Savez-Vous Planter Les Choux?* and *Alouette*. There were also lots of blueberries along the way. Millions of them. We would stop every twenty minutes and eat as many berries as we could. Maman called us her little bear cubs.

But pretty soon, we were getting tired again. It was the steepest part of the trail yet. We were also going above tree line. That's where you are so high in the mountains that trees can't grow. It also meant you could see for miles. You could see the valley we had walked up from Dyea. The Pacific Ocean was now so far away you couldn't see it. There were too many mountains in the way.

It was now getting very rocky. Sometimes, you had to jump from rock to rock. Once I fell and got a nasty cut. It really, really hurt. Maman was quite upset, but Louise knew just what to do. She went to a fir tree[1], popped a little bubble of sap under its bark, and rubbed it into my cut.

"Clean. Heals fast," she said. "You're a brave girl, just like a Tlingit girl."

This made me feel good.

The last part was unbelievably steep. There was no trail, just rocks the size of a horse that had broken off the mountain. This was the famous place where there had been thousands of people lined up to get over the Chilkoot the year before. Finally, we got to the top. We looked back and could see forever.

Even better, we could see for miles into the Yukon.

"We won't have to go uphill anymore," I told Yves. For once, even he seemed happy there wasn't anything more to climb.

We were admiring the view when a sudden gust of wind hit us. It can be very windy in the mountains. I wasn't ready for it and it almost blew me over. Then it started to rain. There were even a few icy snowflakes falling. Actually, they weren't really falling. It was so windy the rain and snow seemed to be going sideways.

"Allons-y!" said Maman. "That means 'Let's go'," I said to Skookum.

We kept going. Even though it was July, there was deep snow everywhere. It was even more slippery with rain and sleet on top. In some places, it is barely melted before it starts to snow again. In other places, the snow never melts.

Skookum told us to stay on the parts of the snow with footsteps. We also had to be careful because it was late in the afternoon. This meant the snow was soft from the sun, especially near the edges where the rocks get warm and melt underneath the snow.

---

1.   Editor's Note: Probably a Sub-alpine Fir, the official tree of the Yukon Territory. It is well known for its medicinal qualities.

We could see big patches of snow that were melted underneath by the rocks. If you walked on something like that, it could collapse underneath you and you could fall onto very sharp rocks.

It's better to cross the Chilkoot in the morning when the snow is still frozen hard from the cold nights.

When we finally got to the summit, we saw a tent with a big British flag. A sign said "North-West Mounted Police." There were a few policeman standing by the tent. In their red coats, they looked more like British soldiers than police. They had rifles and even had a scary looking machine gun set up.

Another policeman in a red uniform came out and squinted into the howling wind. Skookum seemed to know him and called him "Constable." The policeman smiled and replied with a few words in Tlingit, which seemed to please Skookum and Louise.

We were very surprised to hear the Constable speak French to us. He was English, but his French wasn't too bad. I guess he grew up on a farm near Montreal.

He was very proper to us. He was the kind of man who is polite to everybody. Maman was so happy to speak French to an adult.

"We heard you were coming, Madame," said the Constable. "We're so glad you and the kids made it."

"Thank you. It's been much harder than we thought. This is like the *coureurs du bois*[2] one hundred years ago. I had no idea trails like this still existed."

"Well, we'll put you up in one of our tents and I can escort you back to Skagway tomorrow."

Maman got that look in her eye again. I'd been seeing it more often the longer we were in Alaska.

"Monsieur, you misunderstand me. We intend to continue to the Yukon! I don't care how rough the trail is! If Louise can do it, then so can I!"

Aline's Diary #7. Happy Camp. Chilkoot Trail. July 7th, 2006

This is me going over the Golden Stairs. I'm glad my pack only weighed 5 pounds! At the Summit, there weren't any Mounted Police, but Parks Canada gave us some yummy hot soup. Just like Aurore described, I hadn't ever tasted anything better.

– Aline

---

2.   Aurore, do you think your mother could come to class and explain about the *coureurs du bois*? Next month we'll be studying Quebec's early days in the 1700's, including backwoods fur traders like the *coureurs du bois*.—Mr. Galpin

"But you don't have 2000 pounds of supplies to get you through the winter!" We all looked at Skookum's pack. It was all we had left.

Maman stood there in the wind, shouting as loud as she could to tell him how we were robbed in Skagway and had to get to Uncle Thibault's. He looked at us in amazement. "You were there when Frank Reid shot Soapy Smith! Well, where are my manners! Come into our tent and have a cup of tea!"

As we entered the tent, I heard one of the other policemen complain to the Constable about having "Indians in the tent." Louise looked terribly embarrassed. Lots of people in the North are mean to Native People just because they are Native People. It is really terrible.

But the Constable said something sharp to the other policeman and gave him an order, because the policeman suddenly stood straight up and ran off to chop some more wood for us.

The Constable said something friendly to Skookum and Louise in Tlingit and repeated his invitation for all of us to sit around the fire in his tent.

There was a little metal stove, which Yves, Louise and I got as close to as we could. You could actually see the steam coming off D'Artagnan's coat. The Constable saw us inching closer to the stove and laughed. "I bet you kids could use a bowl of beans," he said. "We always keep a pot of beans on the stove for emergencies just like this!" He gave us each a steaming bowl. Plus some bannock to put on top. He also opened up his own box and offered us some Worcestershire Sauce. English people really like Worcestershire Sauce for some reason, but that was the first time we had seen it. Yves said it smelled like rotten socks so we didn't have any. Then we had a cup of tea. It wasn't very strong, but it was nice and hot and he put in a big spoonful of sugar and a lot of canned milk.

I think that was the best lunch I have ever had! When you live in the city, you don't realize how good hot beans and tea are. When you are high in the mountains and have been walking and climbing in the rain all day, there is really nothing better.

We sat there listening to the adults talk in a variety of French, English and Tlingit. More policemen came in to hear about the gunfight, which everyone treated like big news. I remembered what Joe Boyle had said about not letting my adventure go to my head.

Yves and I looked at the pictures hanging from the tent pole. There was a big picture of Queen Victoria and a photograph of the Constable with another tall man with a big moustache.

The Constable saw us and laughed again. "You can thank Queen Victoria for the beans, kids, but it's Superintendent Sam Steele[3] you'll have to thank for the canned milk. In fact, I just used his last can!"

"Who is Superintendentsamsteel?" asked Yves, stuttering over the sounds. He didn't know the word Superintendent and thought it was a name. "Is he a Musketeer?"

The Constable and the other policeman in the room burst out laughing. For some reason, they seemed to think it was the best joke ever told on the Chilkoot Trail.

"Well, don't ever tell the Superintendent this kids, but he is kind of a hero to me too. You know why there are no Soapy Smiths in the Yukon? It's because of Sam Steele. If you steal, cheat or rob, he has one of us arrest you right away. Then he makes you chop wood at the detachment for a few weeks and sends you back across the border to Skagway. It's called a 'blue ticket'."

---

3.   Editor's note: Sam Steele was famous around the world for keeping law and order in the Yukon during the Gold Rush. While Alaska might have been full of thieves and conmen, there were remarkably few crimes in the Yukon thanks to Sam Steele and the North-West Mounted Police. Before the Yukon, Sam Steele had started as a private in the Red River Expedition of 1870. He later commanded police detachments across Western Canada. After the Yukon, he commanded Canadian soldiers in the South African War and was a general in World War I.

"Skookum tumtum," said Skookum. This means he's not just strong, but also brave and determined.

When our tea was finished, the Constable turned to Maman and spoke in French again. "Madame, Superintendent Steele probably won't like this, but you can come into Canada. You'll be safer with your uncle than you will be in Skagway, that's for sure. We've had all kinds of Soapy Smith's gang members trying to get into Canada. We've turned most of them back. Who knows what might happen next in Skagway."[4]

The Constable walked with us for the first thirty minutes into Canada. He told us stories about the Yukon and told us about the next part of the trip to Bennett. Then he stopped, waved "good luck" to us and turned back.

We were walking a few minutes later along the trail, when D'Artagnan barked. I suddenly noticed a shadow on a rock above us. "Bear!" I shouted nervously. But we looked up and saw it was a person.

In fact, it was Blackball. I recognized his laugh just as his arm swung towards us. He was throwing something. Mr. Cicero was right beside him.

The snowball was coming right at me, but I quickly ducked. It just missed my ear as a ducked, but I heard Yves cry out as it hit him in the face.

It was a nasty snowball, with ice inside, and Yves was bleeding from the cheek. I dropped my pack to chase Blackball, but Maman grabbed my arm.

---

4.   Editor's Note: This may explain why the North-West Mounted Police Logbook does not contain the names of Aurore and her family. Every other person who crossed the Chilkoot was recorded. Either the Constable forgot, or he didn't want Superintendent Steele to know he had admitted anyone with less than the required year's worth of supplies.

I looked up to see Blackball cup his hands around his mouth. "Dirty Frogs!" he shouted. Frogs is a mean word the English call us French people.

"He is a terrible boy. I know him," said Louise. "But we should help your brother."

I looked up and watched Blackball run away. I was very angry. Not jumping up and down and screaming but quietly. Kind of like Frank Reid.

Yves was crying, but he was OK. He might have a black eye but nothing worse than a cut. This time, Skookum stopped Louise and sent me instead to find a fir tree and some sap. "You are not a Cheechako any more," he said.

Chapter 8

The Three Musketeers at Bennett

"I guess it wasn't raining when they named this place Happy Camp."

—My diary, Happy Camp on the Chilkoot Trail. July 31, 1898

We reached Happy Camp late. It was a long downhill trail from the summit and we had walked quickly. It rained and blew the whole time. In fact, sometimes we were walking <u>inside</u> the clouds. It was like fog, but with rain everywhere.

Skookum managed to find some dry wood at Happy Camp and we built a little fire. It was just enough to boil some water before the rain got heavier and put out the fire.

"No! I won't eat any more oatmeal!" exclaimed Yves. "Oatmeal is for breakfast, anyway. Not dinner."

Maman explained that Red had taken most of our food and that oatmeal was all we had left. "Je pourrais donner ton bol à Louise, si tu préfères." I think Louise guessed what Maman had said, because she said, "Yves, I would be happy to eat your oatmeal if you are full!"

Yves decided suddenly that he liked oatmeal and started eating. Louise winked at me.

I must admit that I didn't like my oatmeal too much either. I had eaten it for a week straight for breakfast, so having it for dinner wasn't too fun. But even worse, it was raining so hard that my bowl started filling up with water. By the time I took the last bite, it was more like cold oatmeal soup.

That night was miserable. Louise and I couldn't figure out why it was called Happy Camp. Alaska has lots of places with names like Desolation Sound and Dead Horse Gulch. That sort of name would be better for Happy Camp.

I don't think any one slept very well. The wind kept blowing our pole down and water kept pouring onto our sleeping bags. Yves came into my sleeping bag about midnight and we kept each other warm as much as we could.

~   ~   ~

The weather was miserable again the next day as we walked to Lindeman City, but it cleared up at dinner time and got nice and hot. We hung our wet clothes and sleeping bags from trees and had a hot bowl of oatmeal. For some reason, my stomach kept telling me that I really, really wanted a big bowl of pea soup with ham. It's funny when you are in the mountains. Your body seems to know what kind of food you need.

As I told Maman, your body does not always need oatmeal. She said oatmeal was good for my character, although I didn't really understand what she meant.

The next day, we got to Bennett. That's the end of the Chilkoot Trail. We had to say goodbye to Louise and Skookum. That was very sad. Louise gave me a little flower made of moose skin and beads. I didn't have anything for a present...until I remembered my ribbon from Kitty Rockwell. I took it out of my hair and gave it to Louise. She had beautiful long black hair and the ribbon looked very pretty in it. Then I drew a picture in my diary and gave her the page. She drew one for me too. I still have it.

Bennett is smaller than Skagway. People said it was even smaller than it was the year before when all the Gold Rush folks passed through. There were still lots of tents and buildings though. Every tree for a mile was cut down to build log cabins and the big wooden church on the top of the hill.

In Montreal, every different kind of religion has its own church building. But in Bennett, there's just one and everybody shares it.

There is also a great beach. Maman was making arrangements for us to go on a boat to Whitehorse, so Yves, D'Artagnan and I went down to the beach. At first we threw rocks at a log we called "The Battleship," but I hit it first and Yves got really mad at me. "En garde!" he shouted and drew his sword. I grabbed a stick. I kept calling him "Count Rochefort" and he called me "Milady." They are the bad guys in the Three Musketeers.

All of a sudden, a big, deep voice boomed out. "You, sir! You, mademoiselle! Don't you know that the King has made duelling against the law!" Duelling is fighting with swords, and there is a scene in the Three Musketeers where someone says exactly that to the Musketeers. I know the book very well, like I was telling you about before. Yves makes me read it so often to him.

The man had been sitting on a log smoking a pipe, watching us. Now, he stood up. Suddenly, Yves saluted him with his sword. "Superintentendentsamsteel! At your service!" It really was Superintendent Steele. He looked just like a hero from a book, what with his uniform and big moustache.

"You must be D'Artagnan," Superintendent Steele said to Yves.

"No," said Yves. He pointed at our dog. "He's D'Artagnan. I'm Athos!"

Superintendent Steele winked at me. "Of course, you are Athos. Very good." Then he turned to me. "And you must be Mademoiselle Constance."

He knew the Three Musketeers very well. Constance is the Queen's Lady-in-Waiting. Constance is very brave and clever and helps the Queen and the Musketeers outsmart the Cardinal and the other bad guys. "Now, Athos and Constance, you are fighting all wrong. You are holding your sword in your right hand and then turning sideways with your left hand behind you. That was for fancy sword fighting. The Musketeers were <u>real</u> fighters. They used big swords in the right hand. In their left, they had a knife or they just used their cloak." He grabbed a stick in his right hand and swirled his coat around his left. He play-fought with Yves for a moment, then swirled his coat over Yves head. Yves couldn't see anything and just waved his sword in the air. "Gotcha!" said Superintendent Steele.

"Superintendentsamsteel," said Yves, once he get got out from under the coat. "We saw some bad guys."

"Cardinal's guards?" asked Superintendent Steele. He still thought Yves was playing.

"No," I said. "Some of Soapy Smith's gang."

Sam Steele was suddenly serious. "What? On this side of the border?" We quickly told him how we had seen Mr. Cicero and Blackball. He made us describe them exactly. "Well. They are probably using new names. But we'll keep an eye out for them. If you see them again, tell one of my men." He pointed at a tent up the hill. "I'll let them know too."

Then he opened his pocket and pulled out two chocolate bars and gave them to us. "Sit down," he said. "You must be the kids who were with Frank Reid. I want to hear about Soapy Smith's last day. I want to hear it all, especially anything that might let us catch the rest of those criminals. Sometimes I think I should take my men down into Skagway and arrest them all. But I don't think President McKinley would be too happy if I did that. But at the very least we've got to stop them from getting into the Yukon!"

As we talked, I put Yves's chocolate bar into his pocket and shared mine with him and Superintendent Steele. We had eaten the chocolate bars that Tina gave us even before we got to Finnegan's Point and I didn't think we should eat these two in one sitting!

We told our story, stopping to answer Sam Steele's questions. He always wanted to know exactly how someone looked. Was Windy Bill tall or short? Fancy clothes or trapper clothes? Or exactly why they did something, like how Soapy got 300 people to join his committee when everyone knew he was a bad guy. He was very good at questions. Finally, when we were done, he gave us a big Musketeer bow and walked quickly away.

You could tell from his walk that he was a man who was used to long hikes. He went straight up hill into the police tent. As he entered the tent to tell our story to his men, he looked down at us and touched the brim of his hat.

I don't know why, but I suddenly missed Papa more than ever.

~   ~   ~

A few minutes later, Yves and I went up the hill and sat on the steps of the Bennett Church. Well, I actually mean the spot where they were building it. They had just started, and only the bottom of the tower was finished. We couldn't resist the chocolate, so Yves was unwrapping the chocolate bar to share it. Suddenly, Blackball jumped around the corner and snatched the chocolate away. We were completely surprised.

"Give it back!" I said.

"Make me, you stupid Frog!" He had a terrible way of laughing and mocking you when he spoke. "Did you like my snowball?" He took a step towards me.

D'Artagnan jumped forward a half step and growled at him. I'd never seen D'Artagnan growl like that before. It was a real fighting noise. Blackball stopped. He looked like he was scared of dogs.

"Got any more chocolate? You'd better give it if you do," he said. But he didn't move any closer.

"You give that back!" I told him.

"Or what?" he laughed, and took a bite.

All of a sudden, without any warning at all, another boy burst out of the spruce trees. Usually, when boys fight they talk and threaten each other first. Not this boy. Before Blackball could even finish his bite, the boy was on top of him.

"Give it back to them!" shouted the boy. He had knocked Blackball to the ground and was wrestling with him. He was a tall blonde boy, but a few years younger than Blackball. I think if they'd been the same age, the blonde boy would have won for sure.

But Blackball was just too big. The boy had Blackball around the neck, but Blackball got hold of one of the boy's arms and started to twist it back. I realized that Blackball was going to get loose.

I don't know what happened exactly, but suddenly the Three Musketeers saying came into my head. "All for one, and one for all!" I shouted. I grabbed one of Blackball's arms. Yves kicked him in the leg. But then D'Artagnan sank his teeth into Blackball's arm. It was the hand that was twisting the blonde boy's arm. Blackball jumped up, pushed the blonde boy away and ran off.

I picked up a clump of dirt and threw it. It sailed through the air and burst right on Blackball's back as he disappeared into the trees.

"You don't throw like a girl!" exclaimed the blonde boy. He was standing still but was covered with dirt and was panting from exhaustion. His nose was bleeding, but he didn't seem to notice.

"Well, nice to meet you too!" I said. I introduced myself, as well as Yves and D'Artagnan.

"I'm Kip," he said, with a shy smile. He was about a year or two older than me and lived in Whitehorse.

"Thanks for helping us."

"Oh, that's OK. That guy's been bugging me for a couple of days. And when I saw what he was doing to you, I got really mad. My dad says I shouldn't get mad so often."

"Well," I said, "sometimes you need to get mad. That was a good time, I guess!"

Kip smiled a bigger smile. He liked what I had said. I think that was when we became friends.

Suddenly someone shouted "Hey you kids!" at us in a mean voice. It was an old man dressed like a priest, standing in the doorway of the unfinished church. "Kip! Are you fighting again? You know this is a church!" Kip was suddenly quiet. He looked at his feet, but didn't say anything. "I'm going to have to tell your father about this." He turned to go back into the church tower.

Still Kip didn't say anything. That would be so unfair, I thought. "Wait. Kip was only fighting because he saw a bully threatening my brother and me." The priest's lips were still pursed. That means they were pressed together like he was still mad and didn't believe me. I think that's what 'pursed' means. Anyway, it looked like Kip was still going to get into trouble. It's what adults do all the time. They just don't listen to kids. It really made me mad. "You should spend less time giving trouble to nice boys like Kip who help other people and more time chasing kids like Blackball Houlihan."

Then we ran away as fast as we could go.

Kip took us back to the beach to find Maman. "He did catch me fighting three times last week," admitted Kip. "But he's also mad because I beat him in the Bennett Chess Tournament."

Aline's Diary #8. Bennett. End of the Chilkoot Trail. July 8th, 2006

This is us playing on the beach at Bennett where Aurore and Yves met Kip and Superintendent Sam Steele.

As you can see, it's a ghost town today. The things in the water are log pilings, all that's left of the old dock.

— Aline

Fighting Blackball in Bennett where we met Kip by the Old Church

This is a drawing from Aurore's scrapbook, showing how she met Kip. It was when he came to help them when Blackball stole Yves's chocolate bar.

by Aurore

Chapter 9

Uncle Thibault's Ranch

"Is your mum sure she really wants to get off the boat here?"

—My new friend Kip. My diary, Kirkman Creek, Yukon.
August 24, 1898

We found Maman waiting for us near our campsite on the beach. "We found another Musketeer," said Yves as I introduced Kip.

Maman hadn't been able to find us a good boat to go to Whitehorse. There were some men willing to take us, but she didn't think their boat looked very strong.

"You should come with us," said Kip. "My dad is a very good boatman." It took us all a second to realize that he had said it in French.

Kip's dad was named Franchot Dutoit and he was French-Canadian too. He was from New Brunswick and knew all about guiding boats on dangerous rivers.

Nowadays, most people go from Bennett to Whitehorse by stern-wheeler. Those are big steamboats with big wheel-shaped paddles at the back (called the stern) to make the boat go. But that summer there were still a few people who went by small boat. Kip and his dad had just finished building a boat. Some gold miners had hired Kip's dad to float their supplies down to Dawson.

Kip's dad agreed right away. I don't think he'd been able to speak French to anyone except his kids for years. We were very busy packing up the boat. Fortunately, we didn't have much in the way of supplies, or there wouldn't have been room.

The boat was made from Yukon trees which Kip's dad and his friends had cut down and sawed into boards. Then they had built the boat, putting sap and ripped up rope between the boards to keep the water out. Then there was a single mast with a small sail.

First we sailed Bennett Lake to Caribou Crossing, or Carcross as they call it, and then Windy Arm and Tagish Lake. We were really careful on these lakes because they can get windy very fast. Kip's dad said that with kids on board he always stayed close to shore.

But we had good weather. Maman and Kip's dad sat at the back talking about adult things, while Kip told us all about the Yukon and we told him about Montreal and the Three Musketeers.

A couple of times we were passed by sternwheelers. Some were fancy looking and others just looked like barges. But they were fun to watch as their wheels turned and big puffs of black wood smoke came out of their smokestacks. On Tagish Lake, one called the Nora came very close to us, and the people all waved at us, especially the passengers on the top deck who were sitting around admiring the scenery. When the captain noticed us kids, he blew the steam whistle three times to say hello!

As we floated along, Kip taught Yves and me how to play chess. He had a little board with pieces that his dad had carved out of willow. He was very good, but he didn't mind playing slowly so we could learn. He even taught me the Scholar's Mate, which is a way to get checkmate in four moves on adults who don't pay attention when they play with kids.

After Tagish Lake came the Tagish River and then Marsh Lake. Then the Yukon River to Whitehorse.[1] The Yukon River was a strong river. You could feel its power. You didn't seem to be going too fast, until you looked at the trees on the banks and saw them zipping past.

Kip's dad and his two friends steered us very well, either with poles or with big paddles on the back of the boat.

Just up from Whitehorse, we pulled the boat over to the side at a place called Canyon City. There were terrible rapids there in a place called Miles Canyon. Then, just after them, were the White-horse Rapids. Lots of people had been drowned there the year before in the Gold Rush.

We landed at Canyon City. There was a little tramway that Mr. Macauley had built around the rapids. It had wooden tracks and lit-tle cars that were pulled by horses. We unloaded the boat and put the boxes onto the tram car. Sometimes people even put their boat on the tram, but ours was a bit too big.

Kip's dad wouldn't let Maman or any of the kids ride in the boat through Miles Canyon. It was too dangerous. So we loaded the tramcar and then ran to the edge of Miles Canyon. Kip watched nervously as his dad and a friend steered the boat. Kip's dad stood at the back with another fellow, while two others stood at the front very long oars.

"Watch," said Kip. "Now the boat's just floating towards the can-yon. My dad's just steering a tiny bit. But once it gets into the cur-rent..." Suddenly, the boat accelerated as the river pulled it into the canyon. "No going back now."

---

1.   Editor's Note: in the original text, Aurore used the old names: Six Mile River instead of Tagish River, and Lewes River for the part of the Yukon River from Marsh Lake to Lake Laberge. Some writers also referred to Marsh Lake as Mud Lake. Army Beach is on Marsh Lake, which Aurore passed without knowing that she would eventually build her family's cabin there when she grew up. It wouldn't end up being named Army Beach until the US Army arrived to build the Alaska Highway forty years later.

The boat disappeared into huge waves and clouds of spray. Sometimes you could see it. Sometimes not. Kip's dad's oar broke and we all gasped, but he grabbed another and used it to push the boat away from the canyon wall.

"The next bit is the Devil's Punchbowl. It's like a huge bowl in the river and can spin you around so you smash into the walls of the next part."

Fortunately, Kip's dad steered the boat right through the middle and out of sight.

When we got to the end of the tramline, which was just across the river from the town of Whitehorse, we found Kip's dad and the boat waiting. He was soaking wet from the spray but had a big smile on his face.

From there we floated for a few days towards Dawson. The mountains and scenery were beautiful. There was plenty of time to rest and to talk, and we played a lot of chess with Kip. It's a very good game, since it teaches you to think ahead. "Always think two moves ahead," is what Kip told us to do.

I was able to trick Maman into falling for the Scholar's Mate checkmate twice, although the second time she seemed to be paying more attention to Kip's dad than to the game.

The only scary part was Five Fingers Rapids. We "shot" these rapids without stopping. It seemed just as dangerous as Miles Canyon, especially when we passed through with big rock walls all around. Kip said it was really a lot safer than Miles Canyon.

Finally, we were getting near Uncle Thibault's place at Kirkman Creek.

"I don't remember a big ranch at Kirkman Creek," said Kip's dad as he read one of the letters from Uncle Thibault that Maman had with her.

"Maybe it's up the creek a bit," said Kip. "Around the bend, maybe." He didn't sound too hopeful.

"Yeah. Around the bend, I guess," said his father.

It was late and was starting to get a bit darker. By the end of August, you start to have dark nights again in the Yukon. But we spotted Kirkman Creek in time and managed to pull over to the bank. There were a couple of small cabins and a few lazy dogs laying on the dirt by the shore.

"You sure you want to get out here?" asked Kip. I wasn't sure, but Maman was being brave.

"Sure. These people can tell us where Thibault's ranch is," she said confidently. We started unloading our things.

We were standing on the bank, wondering how to find Uncle Thibault's place, when suddenly he appeared. "Aurore! Is that you! I haven't seen you since you were a baby! Yves! Look how big you are!" Then he saw Maman. "Marie! (That's Maman's name) I'm so glad to see you."

He was so friendly and happy to see us. He and Maman hugged. It made us all feel a bit better. Kip and his dad said goodbye. Yves was crying because he liked Kip so much. Every little boy likes to have a big boy around. But I was crying too. And so was Kip, I think. Anyway, he gave me his chess set.

"It might be a long winter," he said. Then he jumped on the boat. They pushed out into the current. "Have a good trip!" shouted Uncle Thibault.

"Marie, come see us if you ever need anything," shouted Kip's dad. "Remember that."

We waved and they were gone in a few seconds.

"So how far is it to the ranch?" I asked Uncle Thibault.

"What? You're here!"

~   ~   ~

Uncle Thibault showed us around. "This is the Lodge." He pointed at a small log cabin, with a grass roof.[2] Not a grass roof like on a tropical island, but with dirt on top with grass growing out. Lots of beautiful Yukon poppies were growing on top. The cabin had a big porch with an overhanging roof. There were lots of axes, saws and animal traps hanging around the porch.

I looked at Maman. I could see she was thinking the same as me. When I read the word "Lodge" in Uncle Thibault's letter, I thought it meant a big country house with lots of bedrooms.

Next was the woodlot. Uncle Thibault chopped a lot of wood to sell to the Sternwheelers.

Then Uncle Thibault showed us what he called the "Back 40." There were some cages with a few chickens and rabbits. "This is where we keep the cattle." He pointed to a large pen with one skinny cow in it. A horse with a big bandage on its leg looked at us and neighed.

"And here is The Guest House! It's all yours!"

It was a cabin just like The Lodge, except a bit smaller and with fewer saws and axes on the front.

It was getting late so we went in. Maman couldn't find the matches in the dark, but you could see where the bed was. She tossed our sleeping bags on top of the bed and we all jumped in. She gave us a big hug and we all lay back to go to sleep.

As I lay there, something seemed funny with the ceiling. It seemed to have little lights on it. I blinked. Suddenly Yves pointed straight up. "Aurore! I saw a shooting star!"

Then we saw a few more. There was a huge hole in the roof!

Even Maman laughed. She said we might as well enjoy the shooting stars.

"If you see a shooting star, you can make a wish," I said.

---

2.   Editor's note: Usually called a "sod roof." They are typical of the Yukon trapper's cabin and are warm and dry if maintained properly. If not, the roof can quickly rot away. A well maintained sod roof can last for decades.

Floating Down the Yukon River with Aurore

Kip

Aline's Diary #9. Bennett. End of the Chilkoot Trail. July 9th, 2006

I went canoeing in Lake Bennett today with some friends who were also on the Chilkoot Trail.

It was very fun, but it was only for an hour. Not days and days like Aurore's boat trip.

We came back to shore when it got windy. It gets windy a lot on Lake Bennett. It would be extra scary in an old-fashioned boat!

— Aline

This is the kind of boat that Kip's dad took Aurore and everybody to Whitehorse in. Believe me, it looks rickety up close!

In the background, you can see the train we rode back to Skagway in.

Maman replied that her wish had already come true. She said she was just happy that the three of us had made it safely to Uncle Thibault's, and that I could think of the next wish. Then she pulled the sleeping bags up over our heads to keep the mosquitoes and rain off us in our new bedroom.

Chapter 10

Seventh Son of a Seventh Son

"Uncle Thibault's magic spells don't seem to work very well."
—My diary, Kirkman Creek, Yukon. September 15, 1898

The next morning, I was the first to wake up. In my dream, a strange witch had been chattering at me and saying "Tsk, tsk" for all the naughty things I had done.

But when I opened my eyes, I was looking straight at a squirrel. It was sitting on the kitchen table on top of an empty tin can. It was eating a spruce cone and making the usual squirrel noises, which I had been hearing in my dream.

The sun was streaming in through the hole in the roof. I could see the cabin for the first time. It had one bed, a table and a wood-stove. I suddenly realized the squirrel was inside our cabin. I sat up.

I guess I surprised the squirrel, since it jumped straight up the wall and started scolding me with that shrill noise they make. When it saw Maman and Yves wake up, it got really mad.

"It thinks we're in its house, not the other way around," said Yves.

We went outside and Maman made us breakfast over a camp-fire.

"Are we staying here?" I asked. Maman said that we had just got there. We weren't going to give up yet. She was being brave again.

There was no sign of Uncle Thibault, so we spent the morning cleaning up The Guest House. It was a mess. Squirrels had been living in there all summer, plus probably a few other animals. The squirrels had been getting spruce cones outside and then bringing them into the cabin to eat. Everything was covered in at least 2 inches of spruce cone chips. Their nest was inside the woodstove.

Yves and I chased away the squirrel inside the woodstove. It was pretty mad at us.

We shovelled out the spruce cone chips and lit a fire to boil water. Yves and I hiked to the creek to get buckets of water. Then Maman made us clean everything.

After that, we checked out the roof. The roof logs didn't look rotten, but the gaps between them were too big and the dirt had fallen through. We went to Uncle Thibault's wood pile and got small and medium sized logs and sticks.

We tied a couple around D'Artagnan's neck and he helped us drag them back to The Guest House.

Maman told us to fill up the gaps between the logs. Then we put buckets of dirt on top. Finally, we patted the dirt down so it wouldn't blow away. I dug up some grass and Yukon poppies from beside the cabin and planted them on top. The sooner you can get grass and flowers growing on your roof, the better. They hold the dirt together and soak up the rain.

You probably guessed already, but Uncle Thibault's place wasn't what a normal person would call a ranch. It wasn't that he was lying to us. In his mind, it really was a ranch. Where we saw a cabin with a broken roof, he saw The Guest House. Where we saw the creek, he saw "The Goldmine."

It was sort of like he could see into the future. Actually, he couldn't see today. Only the future. And not what really was going to happen, but what he wanted to happen.

Kip had told me some stories of miners who spent too much time by themselves. He said they were "bushed" or had "cabin fever." Sometimes they did terrible things. But Uncle Thibault was very nice. He only got annoyed if you said things like "the cow looks sick," instead of "looks like your cattle are having a good year."

Uncle Thibault woke up around noon. We told him about the hole in the roof. He went on a big long story about heavy rains, a bear trying to break into the cabin and how he had a plan to fix it right away.

He didn't actually go look at it though. He seemed relieved when Maman told him we had fixed it.

Uncle Thibault also showed us the cache. Every Yukon cabin has one. The word even comes from French, where it means a place you hide things. In the Yukon, you keep your food in it. It's a little tiny cabin on stilts over your head, with stove pipes around the stilts so no animals can climb up. Uncle Thibault described it this way: "That way no critters eat your dinner." There seemed to be a huge number of critters who wanted to eat your dinner. Bears. Martens. Wolverines. Squirrels. Foxes. And so on.

We settled into a routine. In the morning, Yves and I would fetch water, start the fire and do our chores. I chopped the wood because I was bigger than Yves. Uncle Thibault showed me how to use an axe safely. He made me use a small adult axe because he said little axes like hatchets are dangerous. If you miss the wood, their handles are shorter and they can swing into your leg instead of the ground. He also made me wear my heavy boots when I chopped wood.

Then we would work on The Back 40 feeding the horse or cow. Or on The Farm, which is what Uncle Thibault called his vegetable garden. It was mostly weeds, so pulling them up was our first job.

In the afternoon was schoolwork. Maman made Uncle Thibault build another table for us to work at. She had brought a math, French and history book for each of us plus some blank notebooks.

"I thought Tina put those in the 'Definitely Not' pile in Skagway," Yves said when he saw them. He was annoyed with Maman. He just wanted to go watch the sternwheelers go by on the river or explore the creek. Maman winked at me.

Then, before dinner, we could explore and play with D'Artagnan.

At dinner, we would usually invite Uncle Thibault over. He loved Maman's cooking. After dinner, he would lean back and tell us stories. My favourite was the one about how he was the seventh son of our grandfather, who was also the seventh son of his family. "That means I can cast spells!" he would say. Then he would tell us the kinds of spells he was planning to cast. Finding gold, making the cattle grow faster, putting a second story on The Lodge. The stories were all very good.

We did all this for a couple of weeks. It was fun at first. But you could tell Maman was worried about winter. We would be stuck at Kirkman Creek until May. What if one of us got sick? What if Yves kept refusing to do his studies? What if we got really lonely?

You could tell Maman was thinking about this in September. It was beautiful weather, but it got a bit colder each day and the trees started to change colour. Also, Uncle Thibault started to tell us stories that were a lot different from how he had described things in the letters he used to write to us in Montreal. For example, one night after dinner Uncle Thibault was telling us how he would teach us how to catch rabbits in the winter.

"They're easier to catch in wintertime. You can see their tracks in the snow. You set little traps called snares. In the morning, the rabbits are frozen solid! Like a block of ice! Then you take them back to your cabin and thaw them out."

One of Maman's eyebrows was lifting a little bit. It's what her eyebrow does when something she doesn't approve of is going on. "What do you do with them?" asked Yves eagerly.

"Eat them and make mitts from their fur," continued Uncle Thibault. "But if you're not at your cabin and need to thaw them at your camp, you can always just put one in the foot of your sleeping bag. In the morning, it's nice and soft and easy to skin."

"L'heure du dodo!" said Maman, rather loudly. That means "bedtime." She thanked Uncle Thibault for coming and steered him out the door.

The next day, it all came to a head. That means all the things everyone had been worried about seemed to happen at the same time.

As usual, it was because of Yves. He had become interested in the cache. Uncle Thibault kept talking about how it was full of food for the whole winter from The Farm and The Back 40, not to mention dried salmon from the river and grayling from the creek.

The cache was built to keep critters out. It kept Yves out too, at first. Then he found out where the ladder was.

He told us one day at breakfast. He has a very matter-of-fact tone of voice when he does things like this. "Maman, did you know there's nothing in the cache but some fish and a lot of flies?"

"Quoi?" said Maman. Not only was she so surprised she dropped my oatmeal right in my lap, but she said "quoi" instead of "pardon." "Pardon" is much more proper and she is always telling us to stop saying "quoi."

Anyway, she was so angry she didn't even stop to clean up the oatmeal out of my lap. She stomped right out of The Guest House and went over to The Lodge. It was 9 o'clock, so Uncle Thibault was definitely still asleep. She banged on the door until he woke up.

We watched as she shouted at her brother. "Thibault! La cache est vide! Complètement vide! Qu'est-ce que les enfants vont manger cet hiver?"

"It's not empty, Marie. Why, the kids will have all kinds of smoked salmon and bannock and beans."

"Montre-le moi," she said. Show me. When Maman is worried about us kids, she can be tough. She grabbed him by the arm and dragged him to the cache. When Maman saw inside the cache, she got really angry. She pointed her finger right in his face and let him have it.

"It'll be full soon," he said, looking at Maman's finger right in front of his nose. "As soon as I sell my next load of firewood, we can buy a King's feast!" he exclaimed, getting excited about the future again.

"Tu n'as pas vendu une seule bûche depuis notre arrivée! Rien!" screamed Maman.

"Well, it's true I haven't sold any wood lately. But I've got a big load in The Wood Lot." Unfortunately for Uncle Thibault, at that moment we heard the whistle of a sternwheeler coming around the bend. Maman pointed her finger towards the river and stomped her foot.

Uncle Thibault ran to the river bank and waved. The sternwheeler came around the corner. It was clear it didn't plan to stop at Kirkman Creek. Thibault waved frantically.

"I cast a spell. Seventh son of a seventh son. You must stop!" Still the sternwheeler kept going. It's paddles turned, sending water high into the air. You could see big piles of firewood on its decks.

It was even with the The Lodge. In a minute it would be gone. "Stop!" he cried. "I cast a spell. You have to stop!" The sternwheeler started to turn the corner and go out of sight. Thibault grabbed his shotgun from the porch of The Lodge. He pointed it at the sternwheeler and fired.

A huge boom echoed down the river. But the sternwheeler just kept going.

Thibault turned around to look at Maman.

But she was gone. She was already in The Guest House packing our bags.

Aline's Diary #10. On the train
back to Skagway. July 9th, 2006

I am flipping through Aurore's
scrapbook again. Here is a
picture of Uncle Thibault's
cabin that she drew.

It must have seemed pretty
rough compared to her house in
the big city, Montreal!

Can you imagine how she must
have felt when they found out
the cache was empty of food for
the winter?

Uncle Thibault's Cabin and Cache

by Aurore

This is the kind of sternwheeler
Aurore would have ridden. The
fancy people got to ride on the
upper deck, but everyone else
was below with the dogs and
firewood. You can see the
stairs where she would have
snuck upstairs to spy on Mr.
Cicero.

– Aline

Chapter 11

From Montreal Marie to Kopper Kanyon

"Why did Maman get so upset when the bank manager in Dawson thought she was named Montreal Marie?"
—My diary, on board the sternwheeler SS Canadian, Yukon River. September 19, 1898

"C'est fini," said Maman as we waited on the riverbank. "Nous rentrons à Montréal." She meant that we were giving up and going back to Montreal.

We waited a whole day on the river bank. Maman made me wear the nicest dress I had left. I had a nice hat too that I had snuck into my pack in Skagway. It wasn't the right colour for my dress, but I don't think those things matter so much in the Yukon. Or at least not at Kirkman Creek. Yves was wearing his Three Musketeer hat plus a nice blue cape that Maman had made for him out of a blanket that the squirrels had eaten.

D'Artagnan had been washed and combed.

Finally, we heard another whistle. It was the Nora. I remembered when it passed us on Marsh Lake and the captain blew the whistle. But the Nora didn't seem to plan to stop at Kirkman Creek either.

Maman stood up straight and put her arm in the air. She looked just like one of the rich ladies outside the Montreal train station when they want a carriage driver to pick them up.

To Uncle Thibault's amazement, the whistle blew and we saw the paddles go into reverse right away as the captain steered the boat to the shore. I guess it's not every day a sternwheeler captain sees a lady in a dress, with a little girl and a 6 year old boy in a Three Musketeer costume.

"No, we don't need any firewood, sir," said the Captain to Uncle Thibault. "But you are welcome aboard, ma'am," he said with a smile. The crew put down a plank. We kissed Uncle Thibault. Maman hugged him as if the day before had never happened. We said goodbye and then scrambled onto the ship.

We were at Dawson City the next day. Maman marched us straight to the Bank of Commerce. She had a gold necklace that her mother had given her. She was going to sell it at the bank. Maman wasn't sure how long we would stay in Dawson. She said she might have to get a job to get enough money for tickets back to Montreal.

As we walked through Dawson, it was kind of scary. The city was full of people. It was like Skagway but ten times as big. There was shouting and noise coming out of nearly every building. The streets were full of people and horses and carriages. The streets were made of mud, and the horses and carriages made deep muddy holes. Yves got stuck in mud right over his boots and nearly got run over by a lumber wagon. Several men whistled at Maman.

We nearly ran the last block to the bank. Once inside, everyone was very nice to us. There was a lady in a fancy dress and we waited in line behind her. She had a small leather bag of gold that was getting weighed so she could get money for it. She looked rich.

She smiled at us and pulled some hard candies out of her purse for Yves and me. "Hi sweetie," she said to Yves.

Yves smiled. "You have a lot of gold. Do you wear different clothes when you mine it?"

She laughed. "No honey, I don't. These are the best clothes for getting gold. Come see my show." She smiled at Maman. "The early one probably."

"Here's your money, Miss Rockwell[1]," said the clerk. Suddenly, I realized it was Kitty Rockwell from our ship to Skagway. She looked so fancy, and we looked so dirty, that we hadn't recognized each other.

She gave me a big hug, or at least as much of a hug as she could give me without getting mud all over her dress. She asked all about our adventures. Then she gave us each a dollar. "For more sweets!" It was more money than I'd ever had. Then she smiled and gave her card to Maman. It had her address in fancy letters, and was written on paper that smelled like perfume.

Then she kissed us goodbye and left. I could tell Maman was dying with curiousity about what she had said, but we were next in line with the bank clerk and I didn't have time to translate.

I explained that we had to sell a necklace to get money to go back to Montreal. He said that they usually only bought gold dust. Not very many people brought gold to the Yukon in the shape of necklaces, I guess. But he agreed to buy it.

He filled out a form with Maman's name. "Marie Cossinet, from Montreal." He stopped suddenly and looked up. "Wow! First I meet Klondike Kate, and now Montreal Marie! Are you really Montreal Marie?[2]"

I explained this to Maman in French. "He wants to know if you are really Marie from Montreal."

---

1. Editor's Note: This is Aurore's second meeting with Klondike Kate. This one must have happened after Kate became famous (and rich) in Dawson City, but before she was sentenced to 1 month of hard labour for breaking some of the laws Sam Steele was busy enforcing. Later on, she became wealthy enough to finance the Orpheum Theatre in Dawson City with Alexander Pantages.

Maman smiled and nodded. The man was very impressed. "Montreal Marie. In person. You sure are classier than I expected even in your, err, travelling clothes, if I may say so. My friends love your show at the Palace Grand Theatre. I was going to go next week, if you haven't gone back to Montreal I guess. Maybe we could have dinner or something before you go?" He looked strangely at Yves and me.

I explained all this to Maman. She looked puzzled for a moment, then her jaw dropped and she went completely white. I thought she might slap the man.

The man was disappointed when I said he must be thinking of another Marie from Montreal, since my mother wasn't famous.

We left the bank and headed for the sternwheeler dock.

"Can we go to the Palace Grand and see the other Montreal Marie?" asked Yves.

Maman just pursed her lips and walked faster. She practically dragged Yves and me through the mud down to the ticket office. We got tickets on the first boat out of Dawson City.

~   ~   ~

We waited on the dock for our boat, the SS Canadian. While we waited to leave Dawson, Maman told us the story from the Bible about the towns of Sodom and Gomorrah. I guess they had a gold rush there too in the old days and did a lot of the same bad things that happened in Dawson City.[3]

---

2. Confusing your mother with Montreal Marie. Oh dear.—Mr. Galpin. Editor's Note: Montreal Marie was the subject of one of Robert Service's poems, in which she saves a friend from Windy Bill by letting him hide under her petticoats.
3. Well…never mind.—Mr. Galpin.

Aline's Diary #11. On the train to Skagway. July 9th.

This is Aurore's friend Kitty Rockwell, also known as Klondike Kate. She was probably friends with the real Montreal Marie. Remember when the bank clerk thought Aurore's mother was Montreal Marie and everyone got upset?   — Aline

Photo courtesy of the MacBride Museum (1989-2-261)

Anyway, the SS Canadian was a fancy new boat that had just arrived in the Yukon. They sailed it all the way up the Yukon River from where it goes into the Pacific Ocean near Russia![4]

Most of the people had their own cabins, but to save money we were in Second Class again. Second Class means something different in the Yukon. It would be more like Fifth or Sixth Class in Montreal I think. We slept on the floor in our sleeping bags on the deck where the freight went. Most of the other passengers there were dogs or miners, so the crew stacked the boxes of freight to make a little booth for us. That way we could have a bit of privacy.

The Captain was very nice. He showed Yves and me all around the ship. A sternwheeler is a very interesting place. You should go on one if you get the chance. We started at the bow, which is what they call the front of the ship. The anchor and big winches are there. The winches pull giant steel ropes to help get the ship through Five Fingers Rapids or off an unexpected sandbar in the river. Then there's the boiler. It is huge and red hot. One man's job is to just fill it with wood all day long to keep the engines going. Then there's the kitchen. Right at the back, or stern as they call it, is the pantry. Spray from the paddlewheel goes up in the air and lands on the roof and walls of the pantry. This keeps it cool, which is perfect for the fresh food they store there.

The Captain reached into a big barrel in the pantry and gave us each a huge Dawson carrot. It's sunny all day long in Dawson, so the vegetables are huge! "Don't worry about food on the SS Canadian, kids! Tonight, I'll have the chef bring you and your mama some dinner from the dining room." He pulled a fancy menu out of his pocket. "Tonight we're having Roast Loin of Stewart River Moose with Dawson Potatoes Au Gratin and Yukon Blueberry Pie for dessert!"

Then we went up to the Saloon deck. That's where the First Class passengers have their cabins and dining room. The dining room was lovely, with big windows on the front and both sides of the ship. You could sit in there and see the scenery for miles.

---

4.   Editor's Note: The SS Canadian sailed the Yukon River from 1898 to 1930, when it was damaged by fire. It was sunk on purpose to stop the river current from undercutting the railway tracks. Its boiler was visible until 1997 when it was buried under new road construction. The spot is commemorated just upstream of downtown Whitehorse on the way to Robert Service campground.

We also visited the Captain's Wheelhouse, where they steer the ship. It had a great view, with tall chairs so the Captain could see easily out the windows and down the sides of the ship.

On the way back to Maman, though, something terrible happened. I heard Mr. Cicero's voice!

"What's wrong, miss?" asked the Captain.

"Just seasick I guess," I said.

"Strange," he replied. "No waves around here. But don't worry, I'll get you back to your mama." I put my hand over my face as if I felt ill and quickly walked past the cabin where Mr. Cicero was.

That night, after it was dark, I crawled out of my sleeping bag and crept up to the Saloon Deck. It was pitch dark, except for the spotlights the Captain used at night to see the banks of the river. And for the dining room. Bright lights and laughter spilled out of it. I crawled around on the deck under the windows until I could hear Mr. Cicero's voice.

He was talking to a young woman and an older man. I poked my head up for a moment to see what they looked like. I made sure I did it at a window that was closed and when the Captain's searchlights were on the other side of the ship.

I did that because I knew that when you are inside a brightly lit room, the windows look like mirrors. You can't see out. But they could have seen me if I'd tried to look through an open window with no glass or if the Captain's searchlight made it suddenly bright outside where I was hiding.

The young woman looked like she was about Maman's age. She spoke English with an American accent and wore very nice clothes. They were proper like Maman's, but I think they were more in style. She was also dressed all in black, like Maman's mourning clothes just after Papa died. She must be a widow too!

The man looked like he was her uncle or something.

Mr. Cicero was telling them all about a new copper mine near Whitehorse. "Kopper Kanyon, it's called. With two capital K's," he said. I couldn't understand much of what he said. He used words like "investment," "rich pay dirt this year," and "diversified." I guessed that the widow had lots of money that her husband had left when he died, and that Mr. Cicero wanted to get his hands on it.

The woman would ask questions about mining, but she always seemed to getting things mixed up. Even I already knew that placer gold was the kind of gold you find in creek gravel with a goldpan, and that you get copper from mining the hard rock underground.

The uncle didn't seem to know much more, but he acted like he knew everything.

As for Mr. Cicero, he was always very nice to them, even when they said something silly, just like he was to us in Skagway.

I went back to Maman and told her that since we would be going back to school soon in Montreal, I really wanted to learn my schoolwork. So we mostly stayed on the Second Class deck and worked on exercises. This made her happy and made it less likely that Mr. Cicero would spot us.

Each night, after Maman fell asleep, I would sneak back upstairs and listen again. I almost got caught by the First Mate when he was smoking outside one night. But I spotted him thanks to his cigarette. I didn't overhear much more, except the widow and her uncle talking. It turned out that I was right about her being a widow and inheriting a lot of money.

~   ~   ~

As we came into Whitehorse, Yves and I were standing at the railing. We couldn't wait to see Kip again.

As the SS Canadian came upstream, we suddenly saw Kip on the dock. All the adults were at one end, but Kip was standing at the other. He was standing still with his arms sticking straight out. Meanwhile, a little girl with curly blonde hair and a yellow dress seemed to dance all around him. She went around him three times, fluttering her arms, and then sank to the ground and lay still. I was very curious about what she was doing. I thought she looked like a little fairy, except with no wings.

"That must be Kip's little sister. Her name is Papillon," I told Yves. Papillon is French for butterfly. You pronounce it "Pap-ee-on." I don't know why they named her Papillon instead of Marie or something. But I'm glad they did. It's a very pretty name.

Yves was going to shout, but I told him not to in case Mr. Cicero saw us.

We waited for the First Class passengers to get off. Most of them went across Front Street[5] to the White Pass Hotel. Then we got off.

Kip was very excited to see us. He introduced us to Papillon. "She was making me be a tree so she could pretend to be a leaf falling in Autumn," he said. "She has the biggest imagination in the Yukon."

Papillon smiled. Her blue eyes twinkled shyly at me. She had one dimple on her left cheek, which was like an exclamation point when she smiled. "Kip! I wasn't a leaf! I was the Sunshine Fairy, getting sad and sleepy because summer was over!"

Kip was a good big brother, I thought. A lot of boys would never play with their little sister like that.

Papillon wasn't shy anymore. She held my hand as we talked to Maman. Plus, she seemed to know a lot for a girl who was just a year and a half older than Yves. She spoke French too. "You can take the last boat from Whitehorse to Bennett," she said. "It leaves tomorrow. The railway isn't at Bennett yet, but it's snowy in the mountains already and you can take a dogsled from Bennett to the Summit. Mr. Robinson does it. He calls it the Red Line. Then, they've finished building the train tracks to the Summit, so you could ride it right to Skagway!" We all looked at her for a second. No one was sure what to say. Then she went on, "but I'll be sad if you go. I think Aurore is like a brown-haired forest fairy. She should stay here in the Yukon!"

---

5.   Editor's Note: Known as First Avenue today.

Papillon agreed to take Yves and Maman back to her house to see Kip's dad. They had a nice little house on the edge of White-horse near Sixth Avenue and Steele Street. They had a barn for their horses and a big yard full of firewood. In the summer, Kip's father ran boats down to Dawson but in the winter he cut firewood for the people in Whitehorse.

It looked like it was the kind of wood lot that people actually bought firewood from.

Kip and I kept going with D'Artagnan. The dog had been on his leash for five days on the boat, so he really wanted to run.

Chapter 12

The Devil's Punchbowl

"We can't let Mr. Cicero get away with it again."
—My diary, Whitehorse, Yukon. September 23, 1898

Kip, D'Artagnan and I walked all over town. We happened back to the corner of Front Street and Main Street, just as the young widow and her uncle were coming out of the White Pass Hotel. I couldn't see Mr. Cicero and Blackball anywhere, so I ran up to them.

"You're in danger!" I said. "Mr. Cicero is a con man from Soapy Smith's gang!"

They didn't know what to say at first, but then the widow said, "I'm sorry miss. I don't know any Mr. Cicero." She didn't seem to believe me.

"Oh!" I said in frustration. "I bet he's using a different name now! He's a big old fellow who looks like Santa."

The uncle interrupted me. "Miss, we don't have any time for silly girl's games. Run off now." Then they turned their backs on me and went back into the hotel.

Kip grabbed my arm. "I know who you mean! He calls himself Mr. Clancy now! He looks just like Santa Claus and wears fancy clothes! He owns the Kopper Kanyon mine a few miles out of town."

"The Kopper Kanyon! Exactly!" I exclaimed. "He must be planning to trick that lady out of her money and get out of town on the last boat tomorrow!"

"Looks like she deserves to be tricked," said Kip. "She was pretty rude to you."

"Never mind that. We can't let Mr. Cicero get away with it again!"

"The police won't believe us either. Sam Steele is down in Dawson and the Constable here is really mean."

"But we've got to stop them today!" I said. "How far is it to the Kopper Kanyon?"

We ran along the trail towards Miles Canyon. Breathlessly, I told Kip everything I had heard Mr. Cicero say on the boat. Then Kip and I came up with a plan. D'Artagnan galloped along beside us. There was a sign on the trail for the Kopper Kanyon. It was uphill. The whole trip took us more than an hour. We were pretty tired when we got there, but we left the trail and slipped quietly through the bush. We snuck closer, looking through the leaves.

"Looks like no one is here," I said. We walked out carefully. There were some log cabins with big "Kopper Kanyon" signs on them and a big hole in the side of the mountain. It had little train tracks coming out to a big pile of rocks and dirt.

"Looks like a real mine. Let's go look in the adit," said Kip.

"What's an adit?"

"It's an entrance to a mine. A shaft is a hole that goes straight down. An adit is a hole that goes sideways into a mountain that you can just walk in."

I bent down to pick up something shiny, but Kip grabbed my hand. "Never touch those! They're blasting caps. My friend played with one and it blew his hand off! My Dad says never to go near an adit or touch anything around a mine. It's super dangerous. Rocks can fall on you or an old blasting cap can go off!"

We stepped carefully along the tracks into the adit.

"What's the deal?" I said. "This looks like a real mine. Maybe Mr. Cicero is really doing mining now. Maybe he learned his lesson."

"I don't think so," said Kip. "Look at this! What do you notice about these train tracks?"

I looked at them. Then I realized. "They're rusty!"

"Exactly. No one's been doing any mining here this year. Did Mr. Cicero say they had good paydirt this year?"

"Yes."

"He's lying," we said, both at the same time.

Suddenly, we heard footsteps behind us. It was the widow. "Why look! It's that girl from the hotel," she said. Behind her were her uncle and Mr. Cicero.

"It's a trick," I shouted. "This isn't a real mine and he wants to steal your money just like he stole ours!"

Mr. Cicero pretended to laugh, although I could see in his eyes that he was very angry. "Children! This is no time for kids' games!"

Kip pointed at the tracks. "This is no joke. These rails are rusty. They haven't been used all year." He turned to the widow. "Any gold samples he's shown you are fakes!"

"What's this all about?" said the uncle, turning to Mr. Cicero.

"It's not true!" said Mr. Cicero, starting to get nervous.

"Well, no deal until we get to the bottom of this," said the uncle.

"You won't get away with it this time, Mr. Cicero," I said. "We're going to tell Sam Steele!"

Mr. Cicero roared in anger. I'd never seen him like that. Suddenly, he pulled a gun out of his pocket. "No one's going anywhere!" He pointed the gun right at me. "I'm not getting chased out of town again because of you, missie!" He laughed. "The 'Heroine of Skagway,'" he sneered. That's a word I just learned. It means to say something while laughing in a really mean and nasty way. When I learned it, I knew it was the perfect word for Mr. Cicero. "Well, you're not going to ruin things for me this time. I think it's time for a little accident. A few kids playing with blasting caps. Then boom! and the rocks bury them and a poor widow forever. That would be real sad!"

He moved towards us. D'Artagnan snarled and leaped at him. Right for his throat! But Mr. Cicero used his gun like a club and brought it down hard on D'Artagnan's head. Our dog jumped back. He was bleeding terribly from the mouth and one of his teeth was missing. He kept growling, but he had to back up as Mr. Cicero came closer to us.

"Run!" I said.

"We can't," said Kip. "The tunnel doesn't go any further."

"Stop!" I reached down and grabbed a blasting cap. "I'll throw this!"

"You don't scare me, missie. You'll never throw that. You might kill me, but the whole mine would fall in on your head!" He started walking forward again, watching D'Artagnan carefully as the dog snarled at him. "Told you! You'll never throw it."

I didn't know what to do. What if the mine did blow up?

Mr. Cicero quickly tied a rope around the uncle's hands and then the widow's. He tied the other end to a huge steel drill. Then he picked up some more rope and moved towards us.

"I told you that you'd never throw that blasting cap," he sneered again.

I didn't know what to do, when suddenly I heard Kip shout. "But I'll throw this!" A rock the size of an apple flew past my ear. Kip was a great rock thrower. It hit Mr. Cicero right in the tummy. He gasped and bent over. I grabbed a rock too and hurled it at Mr. Cicero. It hit him right in the hand. His gun dropped to the ground.

He cursed and reached down for it, but D'Artagnan sunk his teeth into Mr. Cicero's arm before he could reach it. D'Artagnan wrestled with Mr. Cicero, never letting go of his arm.

"Aurore! Put down that blasting cap," said Kip. "Carefully!" Then we ran out of the adit and down the trail. We were almost in the forest when D'Artagnan caught up with us. Then we heard Mr. Cicero shouting for Blackball Houlihan. Then a gunshot. I heard the bullet hit the trees above us.

"Run!" I shouted. "Faster!" Kip and I ran like we had never run before. We thought we had lost Mr. Cicero, when suddenly we ran into a clearing. Blackball was on a horse on the other side! I heard him shouting to Mr. Cicero as we dived back into the trees again.

It was horrible being chased by horses. Sometimes, if the forest was dense, we could go faster than them. But if there was any space between the trees they would catch up to us right away.

We ran for what seemed like forever. Kip wanted us to run down steep hills. He said it would be harder for the horses to follow us.

But suddenly, we burst out of the forest and almost ran right into Miles Canyon. Kip, D'Artagnan and I managed to stop just in time. Rocks from my shoes bounced over the edge and disappeared into the whirlpools far below.

"What should we do now?" asked Kip.

Before I could answer, Mr. Cicero and his horse burst out of the forest. "Aha!" he cried. He had his horse's reins in one hand and his gun in another. "No escape now!" We looked for places to run, but we were trapped at the edge of Miles Canyon. "Time for your 'accident' kids! Blackball! Come tie up their hands."

"Do we have to kill them?" said Blackball. He was scared too.

"Blackball, you fool!" snarled Mr. Cicero. "We've got to, now that they've seen us kidnap the widow at the mine!"

"You mean they saw *you* kidnap the widow," said Blackball.

I was shaking with fear. D'Artagnan was standing in front of us, growling and baring his teeth. Mr. Cicero was staring straight at me. He didn't notice Blackball slip quietly into the trees and run away. I looked down at my feet. There was a big wooden plank. I had an idea. "Make sure you think two moves ahead," I thought, just like Kip had taught us in chess.

I held out my hands as if for Mr. Cicero to tie them up. That was my first move. He looked around for Blackball, but Blackball was gone. Mr. Cicero cursed again, then put his gun in his pocket and moved towards us with his rope.

"Tell your dog to shut up!" said Mr. Cicero.

I pretended to shout in French at the dog, but I was really talking to Kip in French. Mr. Cicero spoke some French and might understand, but I spoke as fast as I could and hoped for the best. In English, what I said would have been: "When I count to three, grab this wood and jump into Miles Canyon." The undertow was terrible, but I figured we could ride the plank.

Mr. Cicero shouted again. "I told you to tell your dog to shut up! Don't make me shoot him!"

"OK," I said in English. It was time for our second move...with Mr. Cicero's gun stuck in his pocket thanks to my first one! I looked at Kip and together we counted to three in French. "Un, deux...trois!"

Kip and I grabbed the board and in one quick move we jumped over the side. Mr. Cicero tried to get the gun out of his pocket but he didn't have time. I felt his hand grab at my shoulder as I went over, but he couldn't hold on.

We hit the water hard and disappeared underneath. The water went through your clothes like a knife. It was so cold. I gasped immediately and all the breath went out of me. The current flipped me around like a doll. I managed to hold onto the board, and get back to the surface for a breath, but then the river threw us into the canyon wall. Hard.

Hitting the rock wall banged my hands loose. I saw the board bounce a different direction. Kip reached out for me and our hands touched, but just for a second. Then I was hurtling through the rapids all by myself. Suddenly, it was bright again then, just as suddenly, everything was green and murky. The canyon walls were gone. I tried to swim up to take another deep breath, but a swirling current grabbed at my dress and I felt myself go under.

I was trapped in the Devil's Punchbowl!

I could feel the undertow currents grabbing at my skirt, pulling me down. I don't know how many times I went around. Each time, I would paddle desperately to the top and take a breath, then get pulled back underneath. Sometimes I could see sun, sometimes green murky water, other times just the black depths of the Yukon River.

"A skirt is a stupid thing to go through Miles Canyon in," I remember thinking.

I was so tired. Each time, I had more trouble getting back to the top for a breath.

But the cold was even worse. It seemed to suck all the energy out of me. It was so cold it hurt before it went numb. I knew I was freezing to death, but everything just seemed dreamy. "Don't go to sleep!" I tried to shout to myself, but even under water I could hardly find enough energy to open my eyes.

I don't know what happened, but the next thing I remember was Kip shouting and dragging me out of the water. D'Artagnan was dripping wet and had my sweater in his mouth. I guess he pulled me out.

Suddenly there was a bang. Something zipped through the trees. Then another bang.

"Bullets!" shouted Kip. "He's shooting at us!" I couldn't move my legs. Kip said later that I just lay on the shore, not moving.

He and D'Artagnan dragged me into the forest and the shooting stopped.

D'Artagnan started licking me all over. I hugged him. He was so big and warm. Kip took off my soaking sweater and gave me his. My fingers and toes screamed with pain as they warmed up. It took forever—I don't know how long—but eventually Kip managed to get me to my feet.

We snuck to the edge of the trees. Across the river, we could hear Mr. Cicero shouting at Blackball. But Blackball had run off. Stuck by himself, Mr. Cicero was having the worst tantrum I'd ever seen. Even worse than Yves when he was four years old. Mr. Cicero finally stomped his foot and threw his gun on the ground.

"We'd better find Sam Steele," said Kip, pulling my arm. We started walking and, when I could, running down Mr. Macauley's tramway to Whitehorse.

Aline's Diary #12. Whitehorse. July 10th, 2006

This is a photo of Miles Canyon just before the river goes into the Devil's Punchbowl. You can see how steep the sides were and how fast the water was.

We also found a drawing of the Kopper Kanyon mine by Kip. It shows the spot where Mr. Cicero tried to kidnap them!

     – Aline

Photo courtesy of the MacBride Museum (1989-19-44).

"Any gold samples he has shown you are fake!"

DANGER

←MINE

Kopar Kanyon

kip

Drawing of the Kopper Kanyon mine by Kip. You can see the words on the back side of the paper. Paper was very expensive in the old days, so you always used both sides. The other side of this drawing is a boring letter from Kip's Dad's bank.

Aline's Diary #13. Whitehorse. July 10th, 2006

I went to the MacBride Museum again today. It's a fun place. I even practiced panning for gold with a real gold pan. I asked them about Sam Steele and they gave me this photo. He looks like the kind of person who could really help you if Soapy Smith was chasing you!

— Aline

Photo courtesy of the MacBride Museum. (1989-1-199)

Chapter 13

Superintendent Sam Steele of the North-West Mounted Police

"We'll ground you two later. Right now, let's find Superintendent Steele."

—Kip's dad. My diary, Whitehorse, Yukon. September 23, 1898

One of Mr. Macauley's men took us across the river to Whitehorse. We ran straight to Kip's house and got his dad.

"We'll ground you two later. Right now, let's find Sam Steele." Maman nodded. All six of us plus D'Artagnan started walking to the North-West Mounted Police compound. On the way, I told Kip, Papillon and their dad everything that had happened. Right from Mr. Cicero and his Oddfellows pin to our escape at Miles Canyon.

We were just telling our story to the Constable when Superintendent Steele walked in. "Hello all! I'm back from Dawson. Any news?" he called to his policemen. Then he stopped, turned, and looked at us.

As soon as he heard our story, he sent his men to find Mr. Cicero. "He's probably either galloping for Carcross or planning to float down to Dawson and then into Alaska where we can't get him."

The men came back just five minutes later with Mr. Cicero and Blackball. Mr. Cicero was smiling and telling them jokes.

"He was in the restaurant at the White Pass Hotel having a ham and cheese sandwich and a coffee, sir!" said the Constable.

"Indeed I was, Superintendent. I can't imagine that's against the law, but if there's something else I can help the North-West Mounted Police with, I would be delighted to try." You can see what a good talker Mr. Cicero was.

Superintendent Steele told Mr. Cicero what we had told him.

"Well," said Mr. Cicero with a smile. "I'm glad that's all it is. We can clear this up right away. I did take Madame to the Telegraph Office in Skagway. I was tricked by Soapy Smith too! Terrible man! As for my name, it's Cicero Benjamin Clancy I'm Mr. Clancy. I just let them call me Mr. Cicero because they're French. It sort of got started and it seemed too complicated to explain to them. And as for this story about chasing them into Miles Canyon...well, it's just not true. Who would believe it? Me! Shooting at kids! I'm a respectable businessman. Superintendent, I think we've got a case of over-active imaginations here! That's natural enough for kids. I don't hold anything against them, but I would like to get back to my sandwich."

Superintendent Steele was looking at him. I don't think he believed Mr. Cicero, but he needed some proof. I suddenly realized that Superintendent Steele might have to let Mr. Cicero go.

In fact, I think Mr. Cicero would have got away if he hadn't chosen that moment to straighten his suit and adjust the pin on his jacket.

Superintendent Steele was about to open his mouth, when Papillon's arm shot out. She pointed right at Mr. Cicero's pin. "That's not the red, white and blue pin that Aurore said he was wearing in Skagway. He's got a new one, just like Mr. Galpin at school!"

There was total silence in the room for a minute. Papillon remembered my story perfectly.

"Superintendent!" I said. "Check his cigarette case. I bet he's got fifty more pins in there, including a red, white and blue Oddfellows pin!"

Superintendent Steele reached inside Mr. Cicero's jacket and pulled out a cigarette case. Inside, were dozens of coloured club pins!

One of the policemen pointed at a "Wanted" poster. "It's Masonic Mike!" he shouted.

"No, he's 'Club Pin' Clancy from Chicago!" said another.

"What about Harry 'Handshake' McGintry?"

Superintendent Steele looked sternly at Mr. Cicero. "All of the above, I suspect." He reached inside Mr. Cicero's other pocket and pulled out some tickets. "Looks like you were planning to use the widow's ticket yourself on the last boat out of town tomorrow." He turned to his Constable. "You'd better get up to the Kopper Kanyon. I bet you'll find the widow and her uncle tied up in the mine, just like Aurore says. I'll lock Mr. Cicero and Blackball in jail myself!"

~   ~   ~

After Superintendent Steele congratulated us, and the widow and her uncle had been rescued from Kopper Kanyon mine, we went back to Kip's and Papillon's house. We started cooking a big dinner of moose and baked beans, with lots of bread and butter and a big Yukon cranberry and rhubarb pie for dessert. For some reason, our parents didn't even talk about punishing us for getting in so much trouble.

Kip, Papillon and their Dad got out their special plates and cleared the big dining room table. I guess the three of them were used to eating in the kitchen, but that was too small if you included Maman, Yves and me.

We were just finishing our pie, when Yves opened his mouth. "Why are you sad, Aurore?" My little brother always knows when Maman and I are upset.

A little tear fell down onto my plate. "I'm sad that we're leaving the Yukon. I don't want to catch the last boat tomorrow!" You could see Kip was thinking the same thing. Papillon too. She'd been sitting beside me, telling me stories and holding my hand all through dinner. She even had our dolls sitting together at their own dinner table.

Maman and Kip's dad looked at each other. Kip's dad smiled. "Well, kids. While you guys were out helping Superintendent Steele, Marie and I made a decision. We're going to get married!"

So they got married the very next day, believe it or not. Papillon and I were bridesmaids, even though we didn't have time to get proper dresses. I wore the one I had worn over the Chilkoot and Papillon wore her special yellow Sunday dress. Kip looked very handsome in his Sunday clothes, even though I think he felt silly wearing them. Yves sat beside Kip, with his Three Musketeers hat in one hand and his sword in the other.

The widow and her uncle came too, just before they got on the last boat. They were a lot nicer to us than when we had seen them in front of the hotel. "I'm so sorry I didn't listen to you when you told us about Mr. Clancy...I mean Mr. Cicero!" she said to Kip and me when she saw us. They gave a fancy card and flowers to Maman and Kip's dad. I guess I should call him my step-dad now! And for the kids, they gave us a real encyclopaedia of our own! It didn't actually arrive in the Yukon until the Spring, but they ordered it for us. We were so excited. The only other encyclopaedia in Whitehorse was at the school and Kip said it was missing the letters C and H.

Maman looked very beautiful and our new step-dad had a big smile on his face.

As they walked back out of the church, I suddenly noticed Yves had disappeared. "Where did he go now?" I wondered.

We found out when we left the church. Yves was standing in front of the church with his new friend, Superintendent Steele. They were both in their best uniforms, one blue for the Musketeers and one red for the North-West Mounted Police. And they both had their swords raised in the air, saluting us all.[1]

---

1.   Hard to believe it was the very next day that you started in my class.
      You couldn't even write a single English word! This is a wonderful story,
      Aurore! First Prize.—Mr. Galpin.

Aline's Diary #14. Whitehorse. July 11th, 2006

Well, it's been quite a trip. I spent last night showing my photos to grandmother. She was really interested. I even asked to see some of her photos, which really made her happy.

Together, we picked out these 6 pictures. They are all of Aurore as she grew up in Whitehorse after this story ends. Read what she wrote on each one. Looks like a pretty happy ending to me.

     – Aline

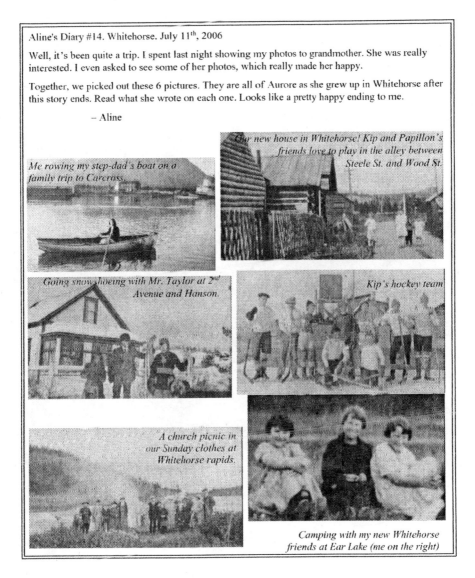

Me rowing my step-dad's boat on a family trip to Carcross.

Our new house in Whitehorse! Kip and Papillon's friends love to play in the alley between Steele St. and Wood St.

Going snowshoeing with Mr. Taylor at 2nd Avenue and Hanson.

Kip's hockey team

A church picnic in our Sunday clothes at Whitehorse rapids.

Camping with my new Whitehorse friends at Ear Lake (me on the right)

About This Book

This book is fiction, but loosely based on a true story and set among true historical events and characters. For example, Soapy Smith, Kitty "Klondike Kate" Rockwell, Sam Steele, Joe Boyle and Frank Reid are all real people. The gunfight between Soapy Smith and Frank Reid really happened on July 8, 1898 as described. But Aurore and her part in the story are invented.

The historical events and characters are portrayed as accurately as possible, based on what we know today. Where it has been necessary to make minor changes to accommodate the story line, these have been noted in Editor's Notes. In the story, for example, Aurore meets Klondike Kate at least a year before the real Klondike Kate moved to the Yukon. The Editor's Note on that page comments on the discrepancy.

Some parts of Aurore's story are based on the real-life story of the author's grandmother Aline Arbour Cyr, later Aline Taylor. The book is dedicated to her and her own amazing adventures in the Yukon.

She was a young girl in Montreal when her father died in 1917. She, her mother Marie Ange and little brother Wilbrod moved to the Yukon to join their uncle at Kirkman Creek. They took the train from Montreal to Vancouver, a ship to Skagway, the train to Whitehorse and went by river to Kirkman Creek. Kirkman Creek was a shock after living in Montreal and they decided to leave the Yukon. They struggled with English speaking ticket agents as portrayed in the story, attempting to get tickets on the S.S. Princess Sophia from Skagway.

Just before departure, however, Aline's mother fell ill and they missed what turned out to be the S.S. Princess Sophia's last voyage. The ship sank off Vanderbilt Reef with all passengers on its way to Vancouver a few days later.

They ended up staying in Whitehorse, where Aline's mother married Antoine (Tony) Cyr, another francophone Yukon pioneer. They lived near Steele Street and Sixth Avenue with their growing family. Aline went to Mr. Galpin's class at Lambert Street School. The photos at the end of the book showing Aurore growing up in Whitehorse are from Aline Taylor's real-life Whitehorse scrapbook.

Aline married Bill Taylor, of the famous Gold Rush era merchants Taylor & Drury, and raised her family in the Yukon. Two of their great-grandchildren, Aline and Kieran Halliday, illustrated this book.

Acknowledgements

The author is grateful to acknowledge the assistance of so many who gave their help so freely.

Aline and Bill Taylor, my grandparents, for filling my life with Yukon stories. The photos of page 113 are from their childhood albums

Aline Halliday, my daughter, for coming up for the idea for this book, and Kieran, Pascale and Ewan for a steady stream of ideas and enthusiasm

Hero, Storm, Zinzan and Tiger Scott in London, and Susan, Noah, Sean and Nicola in Toronto, for early reviews and encouragement

Johanne for tutoring in French

Ken Quong, photographer, for the cover photo

Patricia and Tracey at the MacBride Museum for historical, costume and moral support

Suggestions and proof reading from Grant, Kyle, Charlie, Mary-Ann and many others

ABOUT THE AUTHOR

Keith Halliday is passionate about Yukon history. He was born in the Yukon and raised on stories of the pioneer days. He is a descendent of the Taylors and Drurys, Gold Rush era merchants and fur traders, as well as of Marie Ange Cyr, who moved to the Yukon with Keith's grandmother Aline in 1917 after her husband died in Montreal.

After detours in the diplomatic service in Brussels, study in London and management consulting in Toronto, Keith and his wife Stacy live with their four children in the Yukon, where they intend to stay.

ABOUT THE ILLUSTRATORS

Kieran and Aline Halliday are fifth generation Yukoners. They live with their parents in Whitehorse, not far from the Devil's Punchbowl and the other locations in this book.

They are already working on the pictures for the next adventures of Aurore, Kip, Papillon and Yves.

ABOUT THE MACBRIDE MUSEUM

MacBride Museum is a fun, interactive and educational museum that highlights the overall history of the Yukon. Visit the MacBride on Whitehorse's scenic waterfront at the corner of Wood Street and 1st Avenue.

Look up *www.macbridemuseum.com* to find out more about MacBride Museum's programs, including the chance to relive Aurore's adventures in MacBride Summer Camp for Kids.

Appendix

Women's Supplies for the Klondike According to the Book "Klondike and All About It" By Excelsior Publishing, New York, 1897

"A woman actually needs little in the way of an outfit, presupposing, of course, that she goes with a man who takes the necessary camping outfit and food along. This is what she requires for her personal comfort:

One medicine case, filled on the advice of a good physician
2 pairs of extra-heavy all-wool blankets
1 small pillow
1 fur robe
1 warm shawl
1 fur coat, easy-fitting
3 woolen dresses, with comfortable bodices and skirts knee-length (flannel-lined preferable)
3 pairs of knickers (or bloomers) to match the dresses
3 suits of heavy all-wool underwear
3 warm flannel night-dresses
4 pair of rubber boots
3 gingham aprons that reach from neck to knees,

small roll of flannel, for insoles, wrapping the feet, and bandages
a sewing kit
such toilet articles as are absolutely necessary, including some
skin unguent to protect the face from the icy cold
2 light blouses, or shirt waists, for summer wear
1 oilskin blanket to wrap her effects in (to be secured at Juneau
or St. Michael's)
1 fur cape
2 pairs of fur gloves
2 pairs of surseal moccasins
2 pairs of mucklucks (wet-weather moccasins)"

Visit the MacBride Museum's website at
www.macbridemuseum.com

978-0-595-39546-0
0-595-39546-5